The Purpose

Book Two
of the

The Chronicles of Malachai

By Daniel L. Sweetnam

I would like to say a special 'Thank You' to my wife Daphne; sons, Josiah & Samuel; and mother, Lorraine; for their encouragement, continued support, and many hours of proof-reading, plus editing to help me accomplish my dream to write this book. I also must thank my energetic and joy-filled little dog, Jeremiah, who always encouraged me to take a break, clear my mind and take the time to play a little.

I dedicate this book to all of you and am very thankful God has made you all a part of my life.

To Mac,

Never forget that God has chosen you before you were ever formed to fulfill His purposes here and now. Trust and Believe in His plans for you and don't become distracted by what this world may offer. His way will never fail but you must choose to follow and listen to what He says and then you will achieve the greater purposes with your life that I believe He has for you.

Dan

Chapter One

"The spiritual world exists all around you Malachai. Many people feel or experience the strange and supernatural events this world offers, but since they don't understand it, they don't believe it's real and become confused about what they feel. However, those that do believe often desire more.

The trouble is when it comes to being responsible for what they see or feel they no longer want to listen, they only want the experience and nothing more. Most people choose not to help others with what they learn; they only want to feel powerful and important for themselves. Most will not choose to do what is right but only what makes them feel content. What will you do Malachai?" the angel spoke to me.

I knew this angel well and also knew just how much he cared for me. Many times in my past he had visited both in my dreams and while I was awake. But he always challenged me with thoughts I wasn't sure I wanted to consider. This time, we were standing in a tall grassy field, on the edge of a lake, and even though I knew I was dreaming, the angel's radiance lit up everything around us and brought warmth upon my body. However, the words he spoke cut deep into my very soul.

"I want to do what's right, but I'm scared. The things I see don't seem very incredible or miraculous. They are more from a dark, sinister side of the spiritual world." I replied.

Gently, the angel answered, "There are incredible miracles happening all around you, but your fear of the darkness is blinding you from the greater world which you also exist in. You're not alone Malachai."

"Then why do I feel so alone all the time?" I answered, resignedly.

"Just because you don't always see or feel us, know we are still watching over you. God would never leave you alone, you are very important to Him and He is always with you even when you forget He is there. Sometimes life just becomes hard and the good is overshadowed by the bad. Yet there is always light amidst the darkness if we choose to look for it. Perhaps you need to be the light yourself." The angel finished. Then I woke up.

The next day I took some time to contemplate where my life was going and everything the angel had said in my dream. So as I sat alone on the edge of a cliff that was hanging off the side of a large mountain, I questioned why I was cursed with this responsibility to see these demons and into the hearts of others. Since I was little all I saw were how the demons and angels fought over people to either rule them or set them free. Yet as much as some believed I was given an incredible gift by God, to me it was just too heavy of a burden to bear.

This weekend was supposed to be fun as some new friends I had made from my College program invited several of us up for an end of term party that weekend. However, as much fun as the party was for everyone else, all I felt was my own sorrow and the true pain they hid within their hearts as well. So that morning when our hosts offered to take us on a hike up the mountainside by their house, I was happy to go just to get away from everyone else and spend some time alone.

It didn't take me long to separate myself from the rest of the group as I often went hiking or mountain climbing at home and at camp. Of course the fact that the rest were also still groggy from being up so late with the party definitely slowed them down with hiking. I let them know I wanted to take some time by myself and then went ahead in order to be alone with my thoughts and God.

I'd forgotten how simple it could all really be. So much has happened since that horrible dream in the old saloon with the demon General named Midnight. I had made my choice to fight him and serve God, but I didn't realize then just how much Midnight would make me suffer for it. He hasn't appeared to me for almost a year, yet the dream is still as vivid in my mind as if it had happen only last night. I know he is still watching me and I often feel his presence around me and in my dreams, but he no longer shows himself.

What Midnight promised about the real war beginning was true though. For months I felt bombarded by his attacks. At home, camp, work or even with friends, his minions seemed to show up to make their presence known. Often they took pride with knowing I could see them whispering into the ears of those around me so I could watch how much influence they had.

I did all I could to pray and make them leave people alone, but it seemed like the people would rather have the demons telling them lies then hear the truths God wants them to know. They would rather have power, influence and importance instead of doing what was right. The problem is that I am starting to agree with them again.

All I see and feel is people's anguish, pain, suffering and selfishness; I'm finding it hard to see what is good with life and God's creation. I knew so much truth about why people, the spirits and even myself chose to do all we did, that sorrow and helplessness has taken control over my own thoughts and emotions; I was forgetting who I really was. I was losing hope.

A veil of darkness had begun to overshadow my own heart and depression consumed my hope. I was beginning to understand what Midnight was trying to tell me when he asked why I was trying so hard to watch over people when they didn't really want me to. I was only taking away their fun by reminding them of the truths I thought God wanted them to know. Whether at camp, church or home I found very few that really wanted to seek the truths of God, most just wanted the experience of God and what He had to offer; nothing more.

The more I fought against the demons, the stronger their attack came against those I cared for. Several people I deeply cared for had passed away; many friends and family were going through hard times; and I felt helpless to do anything about it. In fact I was beginning to feel it was my fault for not giving in to Midnight's demands and now his darkness was taking over all I knew with no doorway left for any of us to escape.

I hid as much sorrow and despair as I could behind my mask of humor so others wouldn't see just how desperate I had become. I had also learned how to shut off my abilities in order to protect myself from seeing more of the demons and people's hearts as well. Whenever I did open my heart up to help others, I simply became like a sponge that absorbed their pain, anger and sorrow, but I had no way of dealing with their emotions on top of my own pain; so absorbing theirs only broke my own spirit further. My hope was leaving and bitterness began filling the emptiness.

As I sat on the cliff overlooking a lake pondering all that the angel said to me, I thought about how hopeless I felt and how much I wished for this all to end. I didn't want to be a warrior for God anymore. I didn't want to see the truth. I didn't want to have to care about other people anymore. I just wanted to be normal. I wanted to be like everyone else who just got to take care of themselves and do what they wanted. If I couldn't have it, then I no longer wanted to live, because I just hurt too much.

I looked around the peaceful lake and saw the birds cheerfully flying around singing as they flew. I could see the geese across from me on a beach playing and having fun. Even the fish were jumping and almost skipping across the surface of the water. I used to feel so much peace and joy, but now all I felt was loneliness. The animals all knew where they belonged and found joy in what they did, but it seems that I only exist to serve others and help them find peace and joy. Yet, for some reason it was as if I didn't deserve the same peace and joy for myself.

With tears rolling down my cheek I let out a heavy sigh, and then I rested my head on my knees and prayed.

"Please God, I'm so tired and need your help. I need you to show me why I'm here once again and what you want me to do. I want to give up constantly. I just don't want to be here anymore. I need you to give me hope again or to take me home before I do it myself. Please." I desperately prayed.

Suddenly an overwhelming feeling flooded the entire area and flowed through my spirit itself. A breeze came off the lake and swept up the mountainside and across my body causing the grass and brush around me to sway backwards. I could hear the wind continue to flow up the mountain behind me blowing through the tall trees causing them to shake, whistle and crackle then it circled back towards me once more and calmed down. As the trees and grass around me settled themselves, I heard a voice speak.

"You asked for wisdom and I have been teaching you how to be wise Malachai; but it doesn't come easily." A gentle, yet strong voice spoke.

"Simply having knowledge does not make a person wise. Understanding how that knowledge impacts the greater purpose makes you wise with how you use it. All the knowledge you have gained has brought you only sorrow because you have not yet learned how to use this knowledge for the greater purposes it was designed for. Knowledge gives you the ability to understand how everything exists and works. Understanding gives you the ability to know why everything should exist and work. But wisdom only comes when you know and understand that everything does exist and work, whether or not you know how or understand why; and that you exist with it all too." The voice finished.

"Then teach me more. If this knowledge is only bringing me sorrow because I don't understand why it's happening, then show me why so I can learn what is really going on and know that there is hope for us all in the end." I pleaded.

"You must learn to see deeper into my purposes Malachai, when there is so much sorrow and despair happening within this world, do you not believe that I would have a purpose to bring hope somehow through it all?" He asked.

"I know you must always have a purpose somehow, but how do I see it and understand something so much greater than me?" I responded.

Gently The Voice answered, "Malachai, remember when the little bird sat beside you in your backyard and you were filled with peace? It was then that you understood how within the simplest of things I exist. Now you are learning that within the most complicated moments, I also exist. What does this mean to you Malachai?"

I took a moment to ponder it then said, "I guess it would mean that no matter what is happening whether good or bad, calm or chaotic, you are always there and maybe I need to trust you. Perhaps instead of thinking only about what is happening, I should be looking towards you to understand the purpose of why it is happening."

"Now you are gaining wisdom Malachai. Seek out the greater purpose and you will find hope once more." The voice finished.

As the overwhelming feeling of peace faded slowly away a small bird flew down and sat in front of me. It sang a joyous song and kept its gaze upon me. I lost all sense of time as I simply sat and enjoyed this incredible moment. The last time God sent a bird to me was to bring me hope as I cried out to Him in my backyard. This time the message the little bird brought me was one filled with joy as well.

With one last chirp the little bird finished its song, hopped towards me, then stopped by my feet and looked into my eyes. It passed on a strong sense of peace and joy as it looked at me. All I could do was sit and bask in the incredible feeling the bird gave. Finally, the little bird leaped into the air, opened its wings and circled around me before it flew off towards the lake and out of my sight.

I still felt very confused with exactly what I was to do with my life, but I had found a renewed sense of direction after that weekend. I needed to seek out why events were happening in people's lives, not just try to solve what was immediately happening to them.

I was beginning to realize if a person chose to listen to the demons whispers that brought negative consequences to their lives, perhaps I should stop focusing on what that person was doing wrong and start figuring out why the demon was choosing to influence them in the first place. If the demons were spending so much energy to keep me from understanding my true purpose, then maybe they were doing the same with others. So since I could see the demons then my job should be to stop them.

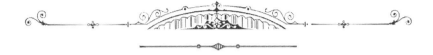

Chapter 2

From the moment I had arrived home from the lake I felt them. They mostly stayed at a distance, but their dark ominous presence surrounded me and the feeling of fear and sorrow began to consume me once more. The demons were again taking note of me and seemed concerned about my renewed sense of hope.

For several days I could faintly hear their whispers and remarks intending to remind me of my worthlessness and failures. Their words came whether I was awake or a sleep; from the shadows and even through the mouths of the people I knew. It was obvious I was following the right path once more because the demons were not happy again. As much as their comments bothered me, it also energized me since I knew they were nervous too and were working harder to get to me.

Lucy and her family had moved to a new house across town from me, almost a year ago now. She and I had spent the day together as we often did, and on my way home I felt a sudden overwhelming darkness flow throughout the area like a thick fog, with the worst of it in front of me.

I could see them, the dark human like figures, scattered along the sidewalks, in mall parking lots and even looking out of car windows around me. They were everywhere, just standing, watching me.

I decided to take a different route home that lead passed the busy downtown, malls, park, and of course my church. I was hoping the demons wouldn't try to attack me with so many other people around and perhaps I could go into the church if I needed to get some help too. But as the people around me increased, the demons seemed to gather more as well. Yet, they only watched me, staring as if to intimidate me and scare me to leave them alone.

As I got close to the church I heard one voice speak that sounded like a thundering of hundreds.

"We are watching you and won't let you interfere. We are everywhere; you can't escape us." The collective voice said.

The voice terrified me, sending chills throughout my body. I didn't know whether to race faster to the church or just get home.

Then I heard another voice, one more familiar to me, one I had heard before.

"Malachai, I haven't forgotten you. I have also been watching you and if you choose this path there will be more of us to fight than you think." She said.

I had slowed down and was a short distance from the church entrance and realized there were no cars along the road, just one person walking down the sidewalk. I looked closely at the lady dressed in red, walking with her head down and eyes closed. Now I knew where the voice came from, it was her the red witch and I was coming to the exact spot where Peter's brother and friends had almost hit her a couple years ago. She was taunting me now.

"What do you want?" I spoke out loud, as I stopped at the crosswalk just before the church.

The red witch began crossing the street in front of me, going towards the church herself; almost to stand between me and where I wanted to go for safety.

As she passed slowly in front of me she looked up, opened her eyes and stared into my soul. Then like before I heard her speak within my head.

"We want you to leave us alone. You don't want this war either and we know it. Why destroy yourself and those you care about because of something you don't even want. If you leave us alone we don't need to bother with you either." She said.

Then she closed her eyes, turned her head and finished crossing the street.

"I don't believe you anymore! Even when I try to leave you alone, you don't leave me; I can hear your words and whispers still. You're making me fight this war whether I want to or not." I answered.

She was now on the sidewalk again and began walking towards the church parking lot.

"Not true Malachai. Your need to be loved, accepted and feel important has caused you to seek us and listen to our words. Perhaps if you truly believed what your God says, you would no longer need to fight us to prove your worth." She replied.

I was still stopped in front of the crosswalk and was very confused by her words. I didn't understand what she meant, but before I could ask she vanished. She was only half way through the large empty parking lot of the church just a moment ago and now she was gone. But I certainly wasn't alone; I could see more demons standing around the area, even by the church.

I decided it might be best to just get home quickly. The church looked empty anyways and I didn't really want to get out of my car at this moment. So, I quickly headed for home, praying the entire way to God for help and protection.

When I arrived home I quickly got out of the car and went straight into my house. I could still see them close by and definitely felt them, but somehow being home made me feel a little safer. For the rest of the night I sat in my room, praying and reading the bible; hoping the demons would just leave me alone. My dog Cassie sat beside the entire time as well. It was obvious she felt them too and was going to stay close to protect me.

As I decided to try and go to sleep I could feel a strong presence directly outside my window, so I began to pray once more out loud. However, an angry voice interrupted my prayer, causing Cassie to get up and begin growling.

"Careful Malachai, he won't protect you from us anymore. Remember what he told you. We have been kind to you for his sake but if you choose to interfere with our business we will destroy you and those you love." The dark spirit spoke.

I could see him through the partially open curtains covering my window. He was partly darkened but had distinctly human figure. However it was his eyes that cut into my soul, they glowed a deep yellow light with a black hollow center that seemed to go straight to the center of his soul.

I took a brief moment to collect my thoughts and then answered, "I thought maybe you had forgotten about me. It's been several weeks without any attention from your kind; I was beginning to feel like I no longer mattered to you. I guess I had simply forgotten what I was supposed to be doing, but now that God has reminded me, you are concerned once more. At least I know I'm on the right track again, otherwise you wouldn't be here."

"DON'T PROVOKE US MALACHAI!" The demon shouted with a thunderous voice that sent a wave of anger and power right through me almost pushing me against my wall.

"We are no longer amused by your attempt to invade our realm. You were Midnights pet that was all. Now that he no longer cares for you we don't have to put up with your contempt. If you continue to pursue us and interfere with our plans, you will quickly learn what Midnight was trying to warn you about." He continued.

I sat down on my bed, confused and frightened; then thought carefully as I answered him back.

"I don't want a war with you. I do understand how powerful you are also. But like I told Midnight, I must do as God commands and will not disobey Him simply because I am afraid of you and what you can do to me. If you and your kind continue to influence or control those around me, then I will do what I must to stop you. But if you leave those around me alone, then I will leave you alone as well." I said, respectfully.

His eyes glared angrily towards me as he began to speak, "You are only a child who is trying to fight a warrior's war, Malachai. We already influence so much around you, even you have listened to our words at times. Perhaps you need to learn how powerful we really are and how helpless you can become. God may be with you, but not all those around you have chosen to listen to Him, have they? You are only one trying to fight against many, are you ready to take responsibility for the casualties you create?"

"What are you talking about? I'm not creating the casualties, you are! I'm willing to leave you alone, so why can you do the same for me?" I anxiously answered.

"Look how quickly you become upset. If you can't handle our words then how do you expect to defend yourself from our actions? Your thoughts are easy for us to see when you have so little control over your anger like this. How can you possibly protect those around you when you can't even protect yourself? Give up Malachai, you can't win." He spoke, smugly.

Maybe he was right; lately all I felt was anger, frustration and sorrow. I couldn't help myself, so how could I help anyone else. If I gave up and quit even trying to fight them, maybe they would leave all those I cared about alone. All I ever really wanted was to be normal like everyone else, and to give up now could actually protect those around me.

Quietly another voice spoke interrupting my moment of self-pity and causing the demon to move backwards away from the window and become nervous again.

"Malachai, remember you are not alone, this fight is not just yours to face." The voice gently said.

From the very depth of my soul, I could feel a warmth begin to grow. I was filling up once more with hope, strength and a remembrance of whom I served.

Boldly I spoke to the demon, "I've heard enough from you. I should have never allowed you to speak this long it only causes confusion and lies. I know you can feel the presence of God here with me, so remember whom you are fighting against when you threaten me. God is who I serve and He is with me always. So if you choose to continue this war, know that I am not alone. In the name of Jesus the Christ, I command you to leave me and those I care about alone. Now go!"

"Very well Malachai, but I'm not alone either. You will have to hunt us all down to keep us from those you care about. God won't interfere if they choose our ways, what will you do then?" He finished, and then vanished.

The feeling of darkness left the room and Cassie finally stopped her growling; then she came close beside me so I could cuddle up to her for comfort. Everything the demon said left me feeling even more confused. He was right, God promised us free will. So if the demons could get people to choose their ways and deny God's, then how could I help them? All I would be doing is fighting back the demons in hopes people will choose God's ways. But how long can I fight them before I give up hope too?

Chapter 3

The next evening my friends and I gathered together for coffee at our favorite restaurant as usual. We were all busy with our own lives now since graduation with work or college, so we tried to get together as often as we could to hang out and catch up on how things had been going. Darren, Matt, Nera, Linda and Lucy all had part or full-time jobs but I had decided to attend College and work at a part-time job as well.

I had always enjoyed spending time working in the garden and with plants. Being out in nature made me feel at peace and working with plants allowed me to let go of my frustrations and let the energy of the plants to calm my spirit. By the time I was sixteen I had already redesigned our townhouse backyard to create a flourishing and productive garden with everything to feed the body, mind and spirit. As a result other people hired me to design yards for them and my landscaping business was born.

It was simple choice for me to attend the new program being offered at the College to teach Ornamental Horticulture. The program would give me all the technical and business training I needed to continue my landscaping business and could lead me to even greater possibilities. The best part was that the regular 2 – 3 year program was condensed down to a full time, everyday one-year program. So I could get all the training and back out working without having to attend school for several years, which was perfect in my mind.

The first half had already finished and my time was immediately filled up with my landscaping business as well as working part time at a local plant nursery. I was also hired on at the camp for the summer to fill part of my practicum for school by working as the camps landscaper and grounds maintenance caretaker. Of course I would also be helping as a counselor, program director and bible study leader as well. I couldn't wait to get back to camp, especially after how the past year had been for me personally.

I was even more excited for camp to come because Lucy was also coming to work this year. She was a little nervous about being a counselor, but everyone knew the real reason she wanted to go was to be closer to her new boyfriend, me. Of course it also meant I would get to spend extra time with her too.

No one was surprised when Lucy and I decided to date. In fact everyone figured it was about time. We had become best friends during our grade twelve year and spent most of our time together anyway. So last summer after graduation, we made it official and our friends were finally relieved they didn't have to keep telling us how much we were meant for each other.

"You do realize that while at camp you guys will have to obey the 'no couples rule', right?" Matt said with a chuckle.

"Yes, I know. But that doesn't mean we can't be friends that go canoeing or on walks together in our spare time." I laughed back.

Dean, Lucy's younger brother, had joined our group of friends recently and easily fit in with his joyful attitude and sense of humor.

"Maybe the rest of us should come to camp too as chaperones for you guys, just to make sure you obey the rules and don't spend too much time together." Dean added.

"Great, with all of you there it will guarantee that I never get any time with Lucy or to do any work at all. So please just stay home and I will promise to behave, okay." I joked back.

Darren also spoke up, "Well at least Matt will be there to keep you both in line and remember Matt, if you need us, just call."

"You guys should know us well enough by now that there is nothing to worry about, after all, look how long it took us to finally date." I joked once again.

Everyone else laughed too, mainly because it was true and we all knew it.

Lucy and I had found a special connection over the past year. We had been friends for several years and become best friends, but Lucy was worried that if she dated her best friend and we broke up, maybe we wouldn't be friends at all anymore. I always understood, but also knew that somehow we were simply meant to be.

Lucy was the one person who was always willing to listen to me. She saw something more within me that she didn't really understand but knew I was destined for something bigger in life. Whenever I shared my dreams or experiences with her, she listened intently and never judged me, no matter how crazy I felt I sounded.

Whenever I looked into her eyes I knew she was right for me and could see that God had given her a special gift too, but she just didn't believe in herself enough either to see it. So for now God had brought us together to help each other believe for the others sake and to be the strength we couldn't find on our own.

Lucy had become an incredible strength for me, but she was also my greatest weakness. She was the one person who truly knew and believed in who I was inside, which made her a target for attack from the demons I fought against. Several times they tried to influence her or cause problems against her and each time I fought back. However, I was quickly learning the toll these attacks were taking on me as after each attack I questioned whether she would be safer and better off without me.

I knew God brought us together and I believed one day we would be married, but could I protect her the rest of my life, was something I just didn't know. For now I felt I needed to take her to camp and experience the time with God that had change so much within me. Maybe she would grow closer to Him as well and discover what I could see within her.

As we left the restaurant and I drove Lucy home, she asked if we could go somewhere to talk, just the two of us.

"Is everything alright Malachai? You seem a little preoccupied since coming back from the lake and I'm just wondering if anything happened that you would like to talk about." Lucy asked.

I thought for a moment and then answered, "I had a good weekend at the lake and actually felt hopeful and energized after God spoke to me, but then another demon came to threaten me, so I'm feeling a little worried once more."

"What did the demon say, how did it threaten you?" Lucy nervously questioned.

"It told me to quit interfering with who they influence or they will attack everyone I care about. Which would also mean you." I replied.

"Oh. I'm not sure what to say, but you do know that God will also watch over us and protect us too. You can't let them intimidate you or else you won't be doing what God wants and they will win." Lucy answered.

I really wanted to tell her everything that had happened, but I knew she was already scared from the thought of a demon trying to attack her personally. So to tell her more details of what happened would only make things worse and perhaps even give the demons an opportunity to create more fear within her. For now I had to keep protecting her from what was really going on. I couldn't tell her just how serious the war had become.

With a smile of reassurance, I spoke, "You're right Lucy. God actually reminded me of the same things. I know He is watching out for you too. In the end I told the demon to go away and God helped me remember how He is always there. I will do what God wants, because it's right and it's the only way to make sure the demons pay attention."

"I'm glad God is on our side and helped you through it too." Lucy said.

"Absolutely, so am I. Besides I couldn't give into them, I'm much too stubborn to let them win." I laughed.

We continued sitting in the car, parked in Lucy's driveway, for over an hour talking when she finally headed inside.

As I drove away I couldn't help but be filled with concern once more because I knew if the demons really wanted to hurt me, Lucy would be the greatest weapon to use. I knew I loved her and we were meant to be together, but what if the demons used her or worse, hurt her in order to make me stop interfering with them.

"I don't want to even think about it right now, please God just protect her." I spoke out loud while driving home.

Chapter 4

Lucy and I both taught a grade five Sunday school class at our church on Sunday. Lucy taught the girl's class and I taught the boy's class. We followed a standard curriculum and were encouraged to do our best to answer any questions students had with sound biblical answers. This was generally easy for me since I had read the bible several times already, taught bible studies, Sunday school and studied as often as I could, everything the bible said.

I also decided early on as a Sunday school teacher to take every question someone asked as important and never to criticize or judge what they said. I was never encouraged to ask the hard questions when I was younger, only judged. So, I was very careful to never do the same to others, especially since several of the students in my class did not come from families who attended church.

David's parents dropped him off at the church for Sunday school almost every week because he loved coming to my classes. He always came with a new question to ask me, partly because he was curious and partly to try and stump me with something tough.

"Malachai, is the devil real and is he still alive?" David asked.

"Yes, he is definitely real and still works hard to influence people even now. The bible has many stories about him and how he tries to deceive people. Even Jesus warns us about listening to him and his lies." I answered.

"Didn't he try to attack Jesus at one point and Jesus kicked his butt?" Robert, another student asked.

I chuckled a little, and then replied. "That's not exactly what happened, but Jesus definitely showed the devil not to mess with him."

I decided to turn to the portion in the bible where the devil tempts Jesus and read the story to the class.

"Now you can see that even Jesus was tempted by the devil, not attacked by him; and how Jesus resisted all he had to offer because Jesus knew what was right. We often want something because it sounds good at the time, but in the long run it will cause us lots of problems. Jesus knew that he came to do God's will, not to simply be popular, rich or famous. Jesus didn't need to show off; he knew he was already important and loved by God. So the devil couldn't use or control him to serve his ways; Jesus was totally devoted to God." I shared.

"But in a way, Jesus did kick the devil's butt still, right?" Robert asked.

"Yes, in a way Jesus did. By resisting everything the devil offered and doing what God says is right, he definitely beat the devil." I said.

"If the devil has been around so long, then where did he come from? Is he God's brother?" David asked.

"He's not God's brother, but God did create him too." I replied.

Robert interrupted. "Why would God create a bad guy though? I thought God was good."

"You have to remember that God's purposes are much bigger than ours. The things we know and understand are only a small piece of what is really going on; and God is the only one who knows it all. God created everything, including all the angels. The angels were created before us and were even there when we were created. Part of their job is to watch over us and guide us to God. However, they're not so different from us and some prefer to do things their own way rather than listen to God. The devil and many other angels were cast out of heaven because they chose to rebel against God's way. But even though God gave them freewill like us, and some choose not to follow Him, like us, God still loves them and has a purpose for them too." I answered.

"How many angels were cast out of heaven? Is that what demons are then?" David questioned.

"The bible says that a third of the angels in heaven followed the devil and all were cast down to the earth and wait here for their final judgment by God. The things we call demons are mostly those fallen angels who lost all their beauty and favor from God, by choosing to rebel against Him." I said.

"So is that why they don't like us then, because they are stuck here on the earth with us?" David inquired.

Robert quickly interrupted, "No, I heard in church that they don't like us because they are mad at God and are now just trying to get revenge by making us not love God."

"Well that's partially true but it is missing some of the bigger picture. In some ways they are jealous because God loves us as much as them. God created the angels first and their job was to take care of God's newer creations, us being one of them. However, some of the angels felt they were better than us and should be worshipped and treated like gods by us too. As a result God judged them in order to remind them who is really in charge and how none of us are meant to be worshipped over the others. We are all His creation and are all His children. We are supposed to work together for His greater purposes not try to rule over one another and make others our slaves." I replied.

"So it's like two brothers fighting over who is their dad's favorite and their dad making them stay in a room together until they work out their differences and start getting along." David said.

"That's an interesting way to put it David, I like it. Sounds like you have some experience with it as well." I said, smiling.

David grinned and said, "Yeah, I've had to spend a little bit of time with my brother on a few occasions, learning how to get along."

"Malachai, what's going to happen with the devil and the other cast out angels then?" Robert asked.

Just then Lucy knocked on the door to the classroom and opened to come inside.

"Hi guys, sorry to interrupt you but Sunday school ended a few minutes ago and some of your parents are here to pick you up already." Lucy said.

"Thanks Lucy. Okay guys maybe we can continue our conversation next Sunday then if you are all interested." I inquired.

Everyone exclaimed with an overwhelming, "YES, definitely."

"Okay class dismissed and I see you next week." I finished.

"Thanks for always answering our questions Malachai. My other teachers were never willing to talk about the things you do." Robert shared.

David quickly added, "Yeah, thanks. I actually get excited about the bible and want to know more about what God says after being in your class."

"That is so awesome you guys, it's why I teach about God. I find it all so interesting and exciting, so I am glad that I can encourage you just the same." I said.

The boys quickly ran down the hallway to meet their parents as Lucy approached me with an inquisitive grin on her face.

"Sounds like quite a class today. You couldn't have followed the lesson because I know my class didn't find it as exciting as yours did." Lucy stated.

"Yeah, we kind of got off topic, but wound up having an incredible conversation just the same. I'll tell you about it on our way to the sanctuary for the service." I answered.

As we walked I shared with Lucy everything my class had discussed and she wished she could have been there. She also thought it would be good to join our two classes together for next Sunday because her class has asked similar questions and she wasn't sure how to answer them. So we began making plans for what to do next week.

Pastor Ron called me Tuesday morning requesting a conference with me that afternoon or evening. His request sounded rather urgent and made me very nervous. So I agreed to meet him at a nearby restaurant later that afternoon.

When I arrived at the restaurant, Pastor Ron, an elder from the church and Robert's parents were already sitting at a table waiting for me. Robert's parents were wealthy and very influential members of the church, so seeing them at the table made me incredibly nervous.

"Glad you could come Malachai. Please sit down." Pastor Ron stated.

I wanted to turn around and run because I could feel their spirits and knew I was in trouble for something. But what really caught my attention was the feeling I had from the moment I'd walked into the restaurant. It was the same feeling of darkness I had during my last encounter with the red witch.

"Am I in trouble for something?" I asked, as I sat down.

"Well, not really. We just have a concern we feel needs to be discussed with you in order to get some clarity." Pastor Ron said, while folding his hands onto the table and leaning a little closer towards Robert's parents.

All I could do was nod my head to give him the okay to continue.

"Did you talk about the devil with your Sunday School class this past week?" Pastor Ron asked.

"Yes. Several of the kids, including Robert, began asking questions about him and I thought it was our responsibility as teachers to answer them with what the bible has to say." I said.

"It is important to answer the children with biblical truths, but there are some subjects we as a church have decided are not appropriate for our children. Discussions about the devil are one of them and we are concerned about what is taught about him and how it is presented." Pastor Ron stated.

"I was very sensitive about what I said and I have taught both in church and camp about the same information many times before. I even taught adults and never had anyone upset with or question what I've taught. I am very careful to teach right from the bible as well. We read the story about how the devil tempted Jesus and then discussed it." I answered.

Robert's dad spoke up for the first time.

"We are not questioning your ability to teach the bible, we just believe that the devil shouldn't be discussed with the children. Only the teachings of Jesus and what is written about him should be taught. The more you teach them about the devil, the more curious they will become about him and soon they will follow his ways. So, we don't want our children learning his evil ways." Robert's dad spoke.

"I'm sorry if I sound insensitive with this, but you just said we should be teaching what Jesus taught and then you are telling me that we should be selective about what is taught. After all, wasn't it Jesus who warned us about the devil, told us who he is; and is the person the story of the temptation is about? If Jesus taught us about the devil and who he is, shouldn't we then teach our young people the truth so they are prepared to resist the devil? Or, perhaps we should just teach them a lie and say the devil doesn't exist or doesn't matter. Pretending a lion doesn't exist when you walk into its den only gets you devoured. However, teaching someone to know the dangers of the lion and to avoid its den will save that person's life." I responded.

"We are not pretending the devil doesn't exist, we just want to wait until they are old enough to understand before we teach them." Robert's dad replied.

"When are they old enough then? Robert was one of the main children asking questions and also sharing information about the devil. So he is learning it from somewhere, but is seeking the truth. He also seems to understand a lot more then you might realize. If you don't want me teaching him, then perhaps you need to before someone else starts teaching him what isn't true. I guess I just believe that if we claim to be teachers of the truth, then we need to be teaching the whole truth. We shouldn't be selective to only teach what we are comfortable with or what aids our personal beliefs." I stated.

"Malachai, you are right. We should be teaching the truths that Jesus taught. He did warn us about the devil and the information is in the bible. However, we do have to respect our members as well and not cause them to stumble either. Can you agree with that?" Pastor Ron inquired.

"Yes, I agree with not causing people to stumble since Jesus taught that as well. But have I caused Robert or anyone else to stumble?" I asked back.

Pastor Ron looked at Robert's parents expecting them to answer.

Robert's dad reluctantly responded. "Well no. Truthfully, Robert came home excited about Sunday school and everything you talked about. He started telling us what you read, your answers and began asking us questions too. He then grabbed his bible and starting looking up more so he could ask you some tougher questions this Sunday."

"So what exactly did I do wrong that Robert didn't understand and might cause him to stumble?" I asked.

"I guess nothing in that regard. However the questions he asked us about the devil, fallen angels and even hell; we didn't know how to answer. I don't think a child should be thinking about things that I don't even understand." Robert's dad said.

With that statement Pastor Ron unfolded his hands and sat back into his chair, and then turned to address Robert's parents.

"I wish you had told me that bit of information sooner, but I am now starting to understand the real issue. Perhaps we need to address some of these questions in our adult bible study so you as parents can have the answers you need to teach your children when they ask. However, when you came to me you accused Malachai of teaching false doctrine and things that were not from the bible. From this discussion I am getting the opinion that what he's teaching is true but perhaps he simply understands different parts of the bible you don't. His job is to teach your children and by his answers today I feel he is knowledgeable about what he is teaching. Can you agree with this?" Pastor Ron spoke to Robert's parents.

"Yes. I guess we owe you an apology Malachai for overreacting. But I'm still not overly comfortable with the devil and demons being taught about in Sunday school." Robert's dad replied.

"Malachai, I apologize for all this too, but we had to know the truth. However, it is still the church's position not to teach things about the devil or demons in any of our children or youth classes unless it is part of our approved curriculum. As much as you are right, we have to abide by our rules until the board of elders decides otherwise. I will mention this to them and leave it up their decision. For now I am asking you to simply stick to teaching the approved curriculum. Can you do that?" Pastor Ron asked.

"I will for now for the sake of these children. But, I don't know how much longer I will remain teaching here though. If we have to censor what the word of God says in order to teach a man-made paraphrased version of the bible then how can we claim we are teaching the true word of God? If the bible can't speak for and defend itself by the very words within it, then how can it really be the truth? I believe God gave us the bible to know and understand who He really is, so as we seek His truth we will find Him. But if I can't teach directly from the bible or answer your children's questions directly from the word of God, then I'm not the right person for this job." I answered.

"Let me discuss this with the board of elders before you make any decisions though. Can you wait at least until then?" Pastor Ron asked.

"Yes, I can do that. But how should I respond to the class this Sunday when they ask more questions the devil and demons?" I said.

Then turning to Robert's parents, I inquired, "How do you want me to answer Robert's questions? Should I tell him to discuss it with you; answer his questions; or ignore them?"

"How about for now just give a short answer and go back to teaching the curriculum for this Sunday. You can tell them we are looking into getting some new curriculum that will help answer their questions, but for now you will stick with what we have." Pastor Ron stated.

Frustrated and annoyed at everything that was being said, I remembered that we are all in the middle of this war and those who aren't against God are still for Him. So, for now I needed to do what was right before God and teaching these children some truth about God was better than walking out and teaching nothing.

"Very well, for now I will do as you ask. But if they do have questions that are not approved to answer in the class, I will compromise by simply telling them where to look in the bible for the answers themselves. I will also encourage them to discuss it with their parents or you Pastor Ron. Does that work at least?" I responded.

Pastor Ron looked at the rest of them, waiting for their nod of approval; then he answered.

"It sounds acceptable for now. I am glad we can all come to a compromise and work this out. Our church values our children greatly and wants to see them successful in their walk with Jesus. Good teachers like you are hard to find Malachai and I appreciate your passion and dedication. I wouldn't want to lose you as a teacher. Thank you for coming and helping us resolve this all." Pastor Ron finished.

"Will you let me know what the board of elders says about it all though? I would really appreciate it." I asked.

"Sure Malachai. Again, thanks for coming out." Pastor Ron replied.

Then he rose up partially from his chair and reached his hand across the table to shake mine, with everyone else quickly following suit and saying their goodbyes to me. It was their not so subtle way of letting me know it was time for me to leave so they could finish the conversation.

As I walked out of the restaurant I could hear the faint whispers of the demons in the background. They had won and they were gloating. I was now restricted with what I taught about them so they could do whatever they wanted. I thought how the meeting might have gone if I told them what I really knew about demons and the devil. But if I had, I think they would have banned me from ever teaching there again. At least this way I could still teach most of the truths of God.

I also knew who all the members of the board of elders were and was confident they would never change any of the curriculum or order more. I had been teaching or helped with teaching in the church for almost ten years and it was always the same basic information. I had also discussed broadening our teaching views with the leaders above me many times and as much as they agreed, they knew it wouldn't change. The basics are comfortable and safe, so we shouldn't change the way things have always been done.

I did what I was told during Sunday school that week and answered everyone's questions as short as I could. I also did my best to encourage them to read the bible for themselves. It wasn't their fault that I couldn't teach them more, so I wasn't going to be rude or angry against them. David and Robert both noticed that I was frustrated though.

"Did you get in trouble because of what I said to my parents Malachai? I knew they were upset." Robert asked.

"Sometimes adults try their best to protect their children by hiding parts of the truth from them. They do it with the right intentions and are not trying to be mean, but they are sometimes afraid that you don't understand enough yet. The important thing is that you seek the truth for yourself. If you really believe you need to know something, then pray, seek and ask until you find the answers. If I have learned anything about God, it's that God will always answer those who truly seek Him. So don't be upset with your parents Robert, instead read the bible and ask God the answers to your questions and maybe you can teach your parents too. Learning about God as a family will only make your family stronger." I answered.

We spent most of the class discussing how to study the bible and which books in the bible are the best places to start reading it. I didn't follow much of the curriculum and worried that I may get in trouble for that now too. However, watching all the children's excitement while they left and said how they couldn't wait until next week, made what I taught worthwhile.

I knew that my time teaching there was coming to an end, so I needed to equip these children with the desire and knowledge to find God's truth themselves. I also knew I would be spending most of the summer working at the camp which would make it a natural time to leave teaching. So with summer break almost here it meant just a couple Sunday's left before I would be back at camp and after all that's happened, I couldn't wait.

Chapter 5

"Have you saved them yet? Any of them at all? Or do they keep stealing your hope and your joy Malachai?" The familiar voice asked.

I had been at camp for several weeks working and felt at peace, like I was where I belonged. The darkness seemed to stay just outside of the camp itself so I felt safe, most of the time. I often saw or felt different spirits watching us, but whenever they entered the camp, I would pray with a couple of others whom I trusted and they always left. However, now I was at home for a couple days to catch up on my responsibilities there.

I knew I was dreaming and was pretty sure I knew who was trying to speak to me; but why, was the real question. I couldn't tell where I was or see anyone else because a thick fog was covering everything I could see. But the sounds in the background and smells in the air all seemed familiar.

"What do you want Midnight? I know you have been watching, but you've left me alone. So what do you want with me now?" I questioned.

"I'm worried about you Malachai. You've been so consumed the last while with trying to do what's right, that you've forgotten how to live. I've seen the attacks you've been under. I even know about the red witch. I've heard about your struggles with your friends, family and even church. I've even heard your prayers to God asking for help with your despair. I haven't forgotten you and hoped you might even ask for my help." Midnight replied.

"Why would I ask for your help after all your threats and what you've put me through?" I exclaimed.

The fog began to lighten and revealed a shadowy figure walking towards me. Other shapes and structures were also becoming clearer and I knew I was inside a building of some sort.

"You wanted to know truth Malachai, and I showed it to you. You sought knowledge and I gave it to you. You wanted power and I taught you what you are capable of. Since I've left you, what have you learned? How have you grown? I may have challenged you, but it made you fight, learn and realize who you are. I even protected you from all the demons who are now trying to destroy you. But now you sit back, do what you're told and do nothing to fight off the attacks." Midnight stated.

I stood for a moment dazed, confused, trying to make sense of what he said. Was he right?

"That's not true; I have worked hard to keep the demons away. I've fought them back from my friends and family. I've learned more about God and His purposes than you ever taught me. I've also become more confident in who I am and what my purpose in life is." I replied.

Walking even closer to me so I could see his face clearly, Midnight asked, "And what exactly is your purpose in life Malachai."

His face was aged and pale. But his stern and serious look is what made me realize he meant business this time.

I quickly composed myself to show no fear; then looked directly into his eyes and answered, "Whatever God needs me to do."

"So God needs you to help those who don't want your help? Or perhaps God needs you to take care of flowers at the camp. Maybe he needs you to teach a curriculum at church that makes people comfortable. Or God wants you to interfere with His other spirits all the time and take away the free will of others. However, I think what God really needs you to do is wish you were dead and didn't have to be responsible for others or His tasks anymore. God needs you to feel hopeless, frustrated and useless. Am I right Malachai?" Midnight stated.

"STOP! Enough already with your lies; you're trying to confuse me like always." I yelled.

Moving even closer towards me, he continued, "You just said you would do whatever God needs you to do. Now you're calling me a liar when I only stated the truth about your own actions. Does God really want you to do all these things or are they what you want to do? Answer me with the truth, oh righteous servant of God."

I didn't know how to answer him. I knew he was right but at the same time it wasn't the whole story. I was trying my best to do God's will but knew that I often wandered from what was right and did my own will. I also knew Midnight was trying to confuse me and cause me to question everything about myself; and it was working. He wanted the truth, which he already seemed to know, so maybe the best option was to speak it, rather than make excuses.

"You're right. Most of what I have been doing is from my own will and desire. I just want people to know God and do what's right so much that I don't always think about what I am doing or what God wants me to do. So you're right I don't really know what my purpose is except to try to understand what God really wants me to do." I answered.

Immediately the fog vanished from around us and I realized we were standing beside the wooden table, on the balcony of the old rustic saloon. The place seemed much busier, with more people and demons around then ever before.

Midnight motioned with his hand for me to sit down on my usual chair. As I did, he moved around the other side of the table and sat in the chair across from me.

"See how lost you are without me Malachai. I left you alone with hopes you might realize it too. Did you even consider that God put me here to help and teach you? You only see me as your enemy, but look how much I have helped and taught you." Midnight spoke.

"I would be lying if I said I didn't miss these little encounters we have, but don't ever think I'm not aware you also have your own hidden agendas. You may have taught me a lot, but so have God and His loyal angels. So if we are having such an honest conversation, please tell me then what exactly you want?" I asked.

"I want you to help me deal with the hypocrites, liars, manipulators and deceivers. Those who claim to be servants of God, yet serve their own ways or the ways of other demons." Midnight answered, with a calm arrogance.

"Hold on a second. Are you asking me to fight against God's people and demons who don't serve you? Or is there some actual noble purpose you really mean?" I responded.

Midnight shifted his position so he could look over the rails of the balcony at the people down below.

"Look at them Malachai, who do you see?" he spoke.

I got up partially from my chair to get a good look at those below us.

"Actually there is lot of people I know down there. People from church, work, camp, neighbors, my family and even friends. But I already know which of them truly believe in God and which don't. I also know who is influenced by demons, some of which serve you. So what's your point?" I said.

"You're already proving my point. You know who is really committed to God and who is just using His name for their own purposes and benefit. You also know which demons serve me and which serve other rulers, and how these demons are influencing people. With so much lying, manipulating and deceitfulness happening around us, wouldn't it be nice to have the truth revealed for once. Those who truly serve God could be rewarded and those who don't could be exposed for what they really are. Would this not please you also Malachai?" He asked, and then motioned to the bartender to bring us some drinks.

Again, he is right. What he is proposing is everything I really desire. I often wished for the ability to expose the lies and deceit of those around me. Even the thought of having Midnights help to fight the other demons excited me. I felt so alone most of the time and even though I knew God was with me, I wished for someone to physically be there too. But was his offer right and would God approve of it. I needed time to pray and seek God's will for this, but what a powerful team we could make if God does mean for it to be.

"I will admit I am intrigued and very interested by your offer. However, what if it isn't right? What if we then become judges over people and spirits that we have no right to judge? If you will allow me the time to seek God's will and approval for it, then I know you're not just trying to deceive me too." I replied.

Midnight calmly got up from his chair and began to walk towards the stairs behind me. However, as he passed by he placed his hand on my left shoulder and I could feel his spirit connect with mine deeper than ever before. I knew his thoughts and heart instantly; he really did care for me.

"Now you know my heart Malachai. Take some time to seek your God's purposes, but I can't wait too long. This war continues whether you choose to fight or not." Midnight finished, and then vanished into the shadows of the stairway behind me.

I was left sitting there alone for several moments listening to the sounds of the many people in the old saloon, before finally waking up alone in my bed once more.

I spent the next couple of days at home praying, thinking about and even considering everything Midnight had said to me in the dream. His offer was tempting, but is that what it really was, a temptation. Was he also genuinely concerned for my well-being or was it just another deception. He still knew everything about me and would certainly know how to lure me back into his ways. However, a large part of me agreed with him and wanted to fight all the injustice I saw as well.

Chapter 6

Ben was the main director at the camp and also my boss for my summer practicum with being groundskeeper. He was a gentle and wise man who reminded me of Uncle Jim and Auntie Jerry. He had been at the camp since before I started going and from the very first time I arrived at the camp he seemed to take me under his wing to guide me. I had learned so much from Ben about being a Godly leader as well as how to understand the bible. He also saw God's hand upon me and encouraged me to seek God and learn how to teach others God's truth.

My short break at home had finished and now I had only three weeks left to work at the camp. I was looking forward to being back and spending time alone with God, but my mind was still very burdened from the dream with Midnight. Obviously Ben could tell something was bothering me as well, since he asked to see me privately shortly after I had returned.

"I am glad you are back Malachai, the gardens and campers have missed you. Did you have a relaxing time off or were you kept busy?" Ben asked.

"It was definitely a busy couple of days trying to catch up; and I sure am happy to be back. I missed the campers too, and the gardens." I said, with a chuckle.

"I just wanted to make sure everything went alright as you've seemed a bit quiet and withdrawn since returning. Are you simply tired or did something else happen?" Ben asked, with a concerned tone.

I wasn't sure how to answer Ben. I had shared a lot about my life with him over the years, but had never told him a lot about my dreams and experiences with the demons or angels. Because he was such a strong man of God, I looked up to him so much as a mentor, so I didn't want to make him think I was crazy and think less of me by telling him about my experiences.

Over the years I did share some of the encounters with demons I'd had at the camp as well as the miracles, answers to prayers and encounters with angels. Ben was always there to pray with me and rejoice at God's great blessings. However, this dream with Midnight was different. I wasn't sure how to explain it, or even how to ask for help with how to answer Midnight.

For now I thought it might be best to just play it safe and at least seek his prayers.

"I am definitely tired from all the work and seeing everyone who missed me, but you're right there is something else bothering me. I had another one of my strange dreams two nights ago and I'm still trying to sort through what it means." I said.

"Is it something I could help you with? You know I'm always here for you if you need someone to talk to. I may not know all the answers, but I will always listen." Ben replied.

"Thanks Ben, I really appreciate it. I'm just having a hard time understanding how to explain the dream right now. But when I get it figured out, I appreciate knowing I can come to you. For now though I could definitely use your prayers." I responded.

"Absolutely. If you would like we could take some time to pray right now then. God knows what's going on and even the meaning of your dream, sometimes we just have to ask for His help." Ben shared.

He was right about God knowing the meaning of my dream already, I just wasn't sure I was ready for the answer yet myself. What if God wanted me to stop interfering with the demons and everyone else's lives, then what point would I have to exist? I wouldn't have any purpose left to my life. I couldn't simply forget everything I had dreamt, seen and experienced. I knew I could never live an ordinary life that was blind to the spiritual world around me. The very thought of God wanting me to stop using my abilities to interfere or help with people's lives scared me.

"Ben, I do have one question you could help me with. Do you ever get tired of dealing with people who say they are Christians yet do very little that is actually Christ-like?" I asked.

"Yes Malachai. I think everyone who truly serves God's purposes gets tired of people who mask their self-serving ways, behind the love of Christ and truth of God. Is that what's bothering you?" Ben replied.

"Sort of. But, what if you had the ability to do something about those kinds of people? Maybe even expose their lies and true motivation. If you knew the truth about why they did things and how they weren't practicing what they preached, would you want to speak it out loud so they couldn't get away with it?" I questioned.

"Would I want to? Yes, of course I would. I'm human and I would love to see those who use and exploit God's love and truths in order to control others or profit themselves, judged and brought to justice. But is it right? Remember we are all God's children and it's His purposes that we should be following, not our own. As much as I would like to bring judgment upon other people for their sins, I don't understand the bigger picture. So what happens if my judgment interferes with God's plan for their life, then God must hold me accountable for the consequences. Are you prepared for that much responsibility over other people's lives?" Ben responded.

"No, I don't think I would want it either. I just find it so hard to sit back and do nothing though. There must be a middle ground somewhere that could protect those earnestly seeking God from those who want to use and control God's words." I said.

Ben gave out a sigh as he leaned back into his chair. Then he took a pause to look around the dining hall we were sitting in. I knew he was taking that moment to pray and ask God for wisdom before he finished answering my questions.

After just a few moments, he straightened himself once more in the chair and spoke.

"Malachai, from the moment of our creation there has always been someone trying to cause us to stumble. The bible is full of stories about humanity and our desire for power, control and wealth. It even shows the same struggle happening in the spiritual realm. So this struggle is nothing new to God. He knows how to handle it. But the greatest stories from the bible that give us hope for something greater and a belief that even the underdog can do great things, are born from the stories showing our greatest evil. As much as it would be wonderful to protect every camper who comes through this place from the evils of the world, how would they learn to see God's grace and mercy?" Ben said.

Then he paused for another moment to look out the window before continuing.

"How can we truly appreciate the sunshine if we haven't experienced enough rain, clouds and storms to realize the warmth and brightness the sun has to offer? Our walk here on this earth is short so God knows just how much rain, clouds and storms it will take for each of us to truly appreciate His sunshine. Some will only see the misery of the rain. Others will try to hide and protect themselves from the storms. There are even those who work hard to convince others of their own greatness for enduring the storms. But God's hope is when we must go through the times of unpleasant weather we will learn to appreciate what it can teach us. The rains can actually water us; the clouds have the ability to shelter or shade us; and the storms can help us dig strong roots. Then when the sun shines upon us once more we can truly appreciate its light and warmth which helps us grow healthy and strong. So, is it our place to interfere with God's process?" Ben asked.

I took several moments to think about everything he said. I even watched out the window beside me and could see how beautifully the sun reflected off the lake, causing millions of dancing streams of light to cover the surface of the waves.

"I understand what you are saying Ben. I guess it comes down to the idea that we are all God's children. So as our Father we need to trust Him to discipline our brothers and sisters, rather than trying to punish them ourselves. But why would God give some people the ability to see the truth of others if they're not supposed to do anything about it?" I questioned.

"Perhaps, God wants them to guide those going astray and to then lead the person towards what is right. If you understand why a person does what they do, wouldn't it give you an advantage for how to guide them to do what they should? It's not what people do that is the problem, but why they choose to do it. What is their motivation, excuse, belief or justification? Where did they learn their reasons for what they do wrong? If someone had the ability to understand these questions, then they will know why a person does what is wrong and can truly lead them to what God's purposes really are." Ben answered.

Again Ben was right. It wasn't the first time I had heard wisdom like this, but I guess I keep forgetting it. The angel had spoken the same words to me only a short while ago, yet I had forgotten so quickly. I still wasn't sure how to answer Midnight, but at least I had a direction now. Perhaps the sun was beginning to shine again.

"Thanks Ben. I really appreciate you taking the time to listen and remind me what is important. After all, if it wasn't for the rains and storms in my life, I wouldn't seek God's sunshine the way I do now. I guess I'm still trying to understand why I do things myself, so thanks for guiding me to what is right." I replied.

Ben gave a reassuring smile, and then said, "You're welcome Malachai. It is my pleasure to be a part of your journey to understanding God's sunshine. God has chosen you to do incredible things for Him, but taking the time to learn how isn't always easy. Just remember, you're not alone in the journey."

I gave him a big hug and then we left to carry on our duties for the week of camp. I would be taking care of the grounds while also teaching activities and bible studies. So with a beginning to a week like this, I knew God would have exciting things to teach through me since I was already learning so much.

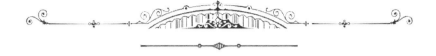

Chapter 7

The week at camp had gone so fast and God was definitely doing amazing things in people's lives, both campers and staff. My bible studies even had a renewed energy to them. I was excited to be teaching about God's hope, love and purpose for us all. Everything seemed to work perfectly together from crafts, skits, games, bible studies, activities and even campfire, everything that happened supported the message God was trying to tell us.

The message was reminding us how we each have an important ability that we are good at and when we trust God to guide us with it we can do amazing things. Then, if we are willing to use that ability to work with, support and help others, we help them grow and cause ourselves to grow also. We all took the time to listen and learn from each other; even the campers had much to teach us staff. The result was a powerful life-changing week with God in control.

Of course for me the week was made even better by the fact that Lucy was there with me. This was her first week coming to camp and was definitely a great week for her to be there.

"I can't believe how fast the week goes now that I am at camp. When you are here and I'm at home it seems to take forever and I can't wait for you to get back. But, we are so busy here that it goes so fast and now I don't want it to end." Lucy said.

"At least you can understand why I love it here so much now. It's an incredible experience to be a part of God's plans for helping others and how He uses our skills to change the lives of others and our own. I'm so glad you could be here with me for this week in particular. It was an amazing week, but having you here made it even better." I shared.

Lucy took my hand in hers, then smiled and said, "I'm glad I was here to spend it with you too Malachai and I definitely want to come back next year. I got to spend more time with you, make new friends and share some of what God's done in my life with the campers. The best part was that they loved hearing about it."

"Okay you love birds, camps not over with yet, so remember, NO Dating." Matt interrupted us, while laughing.

"Uhmm, we were only holding hands in order to pray with each other." I joked.

"Yah, yah. God knows the truth and you can't fool me either." Matt chuckled, and then continued. "Anyways, I just wanted to let you know that your mom is here looking for you, Malachai. I told her she could wait in the dining hall and I would find you, and then send you there."

"Oh, I wonder why she's here. I guess she misses me. I am a very loveable person. Right Lucy?" I asked.

"Sure you are, umm, yep very loveable." She answered, while both her and Matt giggled the whole time.

"Just kidding, Malachai. Of course you are loveable. You go find your mom and I will go say goodbye to my campers and finish packing. I will catch up with you in a bit. Bye my loveable Malachai." She said, still giggling.

As Matt and Lucy left and I began walking towards the dining hall to see my mom. Suddenly a heavy feeling came upon me and the air grew thick and hard to breath. The sun that was shining around me became grayed like at dusk and a hazy film seemed to cover everywhere I looked.

"It's not too late Malachai, but time is running out." Came the voice from behind the trees on the side of the driveway.

As he stepped out from amidst the trees, I could see him very clearly. It was Midnight, dressed in his long black coat, black shirt, black pants and his unforgettable pale white face.

"I came to see if you had made a decision yet Malachai. I can't wait much longer and I can't stop the others from doing what they feel is necessary." Midnight said.

"What do you mean? Who wants to do what?" I asked.

"I warned you that we are in a war and because God granted you your ability to see us, it has made you a target to destroy. I have tried to guide you, teach you and urge you to join me to fight against them, but it seems you just want to remain neutral and do nothing." He answered.

"That's not true. I just won't decide to fight the war your way. I serve God and I'm trying to see His will for what I should do. If He wants me to help you, then I will. But if He doesn't, there must be a good reason why. Now tell me why you are here, what's going on?" I asked again.

"Your life is about to change once more Malachai. They influence way more than you can imagine and they have been shaping your life circumstances in order to bring your destruction. If it weren't for my interventions, they most certainly would have succeeded too. They give people what they want knowing it will only cause them to grow further from what they really need and what they should be doing. But even though they have influenced your life again, if you choose to join me now, I will guide you and keep you safe from their larger attack." Midnight replied.

"I just had one of the most amazing weeks here at camp. God is doing incredible things in my life and through me this week. So I don't understand what the attack you are talking about is. Perhaps you are just trying to confuse me again and destroy the joy I'm feeling after such an awesome week." I answered.

"Malachai open your eyes. You have far worse enemies to worry about than me right now. One little ripple of change in a person's life can have so many consequences. You have been way too busy interfering in other spirit's realm of influence. So now you are about to be kept too busy to be a problem much more. You are right, someone is trying to steal your joy, but it isn't me. However, I can help you fight back and stop their plans. But you have to do it my way." He said.

After speaking these words, Midnight's form quickly changed into a shadowy fog that faded from black, to gray; then disappeared completely.

Only seconds had passed since Midnight finished speaking when I was interrupted by Matt's voice.

"Malachai, why are you standing there? Your mom is still waiting for you in the dining hall. You better hurry up." Matt yelled to me from the top of the driveway.

I took a moment to gather my thoughts; then answered.
"I'll be right there Matt. Thanks." I replied.

I looked around for any sign or feeling of Midnight, but he was definitely gone; for now at least. Whatever he was talking about obviously had something to do with why my mom was here at camp. But I wish he had told me what the attack was so I knew what to do about it. I guess the only way to find out was to go meet my mom.

As I entered the dining hall my mom was sitting with Ben at a table close to the windows overlooking the lake. I could hear them talking about me, and Ben was telling her how much he appreciated what I did at camp and could sense God's anointing on my life.

When my mom noticed me she got up from her chair to give me a hug.

"I was beginning to wonder what happened to you. Thankfully Ben was here though, which gave us a chance to catch up on how you have been behaving this summer." My mom said.

"Should I be worried about what Ben might be telling you?" I joked.

Ben quickly answered, "Don't worry Malachai, I only told her the good stuff. I want to make sure you stay for the last week of camp. So I figured I would be nice."

"Thanks Ben, I appreciate you covering for me." I said, with a chuckle.

"You're welcome. I'll leave you two alone and get back to my own work." Ben replied.

My mom turned to me and said, "I don't have too much time, but I have some news that I wanted to tell you in person. I sold the house on Thursday and we need to move by the end of September."

My heart sank and so many questions began filling my head that I didn't know where to begin.

"What are you talking about? The house wasn't for sale and it's the end of August. Where are we supposed to live?" I answered, panicked.

"I know it's a shock Malachai. It all just happened so fast. A realtor came by a few days ago trying to get some listings in our townhouse complex and asked if I was interested in selling. I told him that I wasn't interested, but jokingly said for the right price I might change my mind. So he asked me how much I wanted. I threw a high number out there figuring no one would ever take it. Well on Thursday he came back and said he had a buyer that will pay what I wanted." My mom said.

"What are we supposed to do now though? Where will we live when we only have a month to move out of the house that we have lived in most of my life? Why did you say yes?" I asked.

My mom sat down at the table and continued.

"Well I'm not working right now and could certainly use the money. Your one brother is planning to move out soon anyways. You'll be finishing College this fall and then want to move on with your own life. Your oldest brother and his family just moved to the Okanagan and want me to go up there too. So, I just feel God is opening a door for me and that He wants me to sell it. I know you will be fine and that God will take care of you too. He always does." She answered.

"I don't know what to say, I'm in shock. I guess I'll just have to figure out what to do when I get home then. I still have one more week to work here at camp before I can come home and now I'll need the money in order to pay for a new place to live. Plus, I have school starting up again in a couple weeks. So I can't say I'm happy about it because it's just not very good timing for me to even pack everything. But I guess I'll just have to trust God to work it all out." I replied.

"We will all have some big adjustments to make, but it just seems like God has opened the door and I feel I need to take it. I hope you can understand. Anyways, I'm sorry I can't stay longer but I have to get back to start getting the paperwork organized. I just wanted to come up and tell you in person. I'll see you in a week then, okay." My mom stated, as she was getting up to leave already.

"Fine. I guess I'll see you in a week." I answered, and then gave her a hug before she left.

I was confused, shocked, angry and exhausted from the news. This was what Midnight meant by the attack from the other demons. One moment my life was filled with joy and excitement from a great week at camp. The next moment I'm filled with anger, confusion and despair. But what could I do, it was out of my hands and wasn't my choice.

Just then Ben walked back into the dining hall and noticed me blankly staring out the window.

"Is everything alright Malachai? Did your mom bring some bad news?" Ben asked.

I was trying hard to hold back my tears, so decided to keep staring out the window while I answered him.

"Yeah, kind of. It will certainly change my life once more." I said.

"Do you want to sit down and talk about it?" Ben inquired.

"Actually, I think that might be a good idea. I'm pretty frustrated right now and it might help to talk about it before it destroys everything God did this past week." I replied.

Ben and I talked for quite a while as I shared everything that my mom said and exactly how I felt about it all. He offered some great advice and after I was finished we took some time to pray and seek God's help for what to do next.

I didn't tell Ben about my encounter with Midnight and what he had said to me. But it all sat heavily upon my heart. Midnight said I would be so busy that I couldn't interfere with the other demons plans and it looks like he was right. He also said he would help me fight those demons, which I could definitely use help with now. But, was it right and would God approve of me working with Midnight to fight this war. I just wished I knew what to do.

For now I knew I had to finish my final week at camp; then I could go home to figure out where I will live and work while I finish my last semester of school. At least Midnight warned me that something was about to happen, so I know this is just another attack. Perhaps if I keep doing what God wants me to do regardless of what others do, He will make it all work out for me in the end. I just needed to trust Him once again.

Thanks to Midnight, I also know the demons plans of wanting me out of their way and keeping me so busy that I can't interfere with what they are doing. At the very least it gives me an advantage to be careful of my own choices and to make the time to hear whatever God needs me to do. The more I thought about it, I actually felt a little flattered that I have been doing such a good job in fighting these demons that they felt the need to get me out of their way. It was an interesting thought anyways.

Chapter 8

The final week of camp went fast and I was consumed with the worry about my own future. God continued to work His miracles and purposes in everyone's lives throughout the week; however, I just couldn't find the joy because of what I'd have to face when I went home. My friends tried to encourage me and pray for me, so I did my best to put on a smile and continue for their sake. Yet, inside I was afraid and wished I could remain at camp forever.

As I prepared to leave for home Ben called me over and asked me to walk with him down to the beach on the edge of the lake.

"Malachai, I can't say I know what plans God has for you exactly, however I do know if you trust your plans into His hands, He will take care of you. Take a look around this beach and see how beautiful all the gardens, lawns and trees are looking. I took a chance to trust God's plans for the camp this summer and I hired you to care for these grounds. I watched as you weeded, tilled, pruned and cared for everything you saw and how you prayed over all of it.

The result is obvious; God has blessed everything you've done." Ben began saying.

"That means a lot to me Ben. I loved being here and appreciate the opportunity." I shared.

Ben looked towards the lake and then continued.

"I've also noticed how you take the same care and prayer when you teach God's word, lead cabin groups, activities, wash dishes or even pray for others. You have a real calling to lead the hearts of others to the heart of God, and you live it, not simply speak it. I want you know I can see your passion for God and every task I've given you, God's blessing has been with you. It's quite remarkable to watch. So even though I don't know what God has planned for your future, I am sure that if you keep following His ways He will bless whatever you do."

I wasn't sure what to say. His words meant a lot to me and his heart was sincere and full of compassion for me.

"Thank you Ben. To know how much you believe in me gives me strength. I wish I knew exactly what the future held for me, but it does help to know I have someone who is praying and believes in me even when I'm having trouble." I said.

"If I can ever do anything to help, please let me know. And I will be praying for you always." Ben replied.

I said my final goodbyes to my friends that were still lingering around the camp and of course took one last moment with God down by the lake, and then it was time to face whatever was to come at home. I wasn't anxious to get home, but stalling the inevitable wasn't the answer either. So with one last deep sigh, I climbed into my car and left for home, at least what I will call home for the next month.

Midnight was right about the demons desire to keep me far too busy to interfere with their lives. From the moment I returned home from camp my life had become a whirlwind of confusion and busyness. God was still in control of my life, but there were so many decisions and jobs to do that I barely had the time to pray or think.

With much work and help from Lucy and Nera we got the house packed, cleaned and ready to move out. God had even provided an apartment for my one brother and I to live in which was brand new and not noted for allowing young people like our selves to live there. The apartment was generally for middle aged financially secure people, not young adults just starting off in life.

"Normally it's not our policy to allow young people to rent in the building on their own because we are concerned with noise and respectability for others. We don't tolerate loud partying or careless behavior both in and around the apartments. However, you had a very good reference who assured me of the kind of person you are Malachai and that I could trust you to be good tenants. So, you have been allowed here because of his support." The manager said.

I was surprised by his words and honored at the same time. But I definitely needed to know who had talked to him.

"We are very grateful that you have allowed us to live here, it is a beautiful apartment. But may I ask who it was that gave such a good reference to cause you to consider changing your policy?" I questioned.

"Sure I can tell you. He's actually a very close friend of mine who cares a great deal about you Malachai. It's Ben. When I saw on your application you had worked at the camp, I thought I would call him up and get his opinion of you. He thinks very highly of you and let me know how much you needed a good, safe place to stay. So, after meeting you both the other day I could agree with Ben's opinion. Welcome to the building." He shared.

"Again, thank you so much. I will have to thank Ben too, he is an incredible person." I stated.

It was very reassuring to know that God was looking out for me still and so was Ben.

After finishing the move to our new apartment and saying goodbye to my home of seventeen years, the next stage of life had begun. Between school, working several part-time jobs, Lucy and friends; time flew by incredibly fast and change became the one constant in my life.

My mom had moved with my oldest brother, several hours away. Plus, my other brother decided to move in with his best friend, leaving me with the apartment and expenses on my own. So, thankfully I had graduated from my college program already and had taken almost full-time work at a department store by working in several different departments, to help get the hours and pay I needed.

I had very little time to care about the spiritual war I still saw around me and I was far too tired to fight any demons. I always took the time to pray for those closest to me and did my best to watch over them. But, when it came to strangers and other people I knew, I often said a quick prayer for God to help them and then continued on with my own life. I simply didn't have the energy left to watch over any more people.

"I warned you Malachai, the others wouldn't tolerate your interference any longer and you would be powerless to fight them without me. They are playing on your humanness. Your kind are so easily distracted from what really matters by the need for your own security. By making you insecure, uncomfortable or lacking in your daily comforts; you work much harder to earn your comfort back and you'll let everything else slide." I heard Midnight speak.

I was sitting in the old wooden saloon once again but this time I wasn't sitting up above at my usual table. This time I was sitting at one of the dirty, stained tables on the floor below. The second wooden staircase leading up to the balcony, Midnight's private staircase, was directly behind me. Beside me were the swinging wooden doors leading to the back room where the demons waited until needed by their patrons in the main room.

The floor around me was disgusting, covered with broken bottles, glasses, needles, garbage, vomit and blood. The fire I saw burning before from underneath the wooden boards was much brighter from here. I could hear the fires crackling and even feel its warmth.

My table was very worn with many cuts and scratches on its surface. There were still puddles of alcohol strewn across the surface and a glass tipped on its side, obviously left from the previous visitor to this table.

The servers were very busy walking in and out of the room beside me. The place was busier than usual and there was a lot of work for these demons to do. However, none of them seemed to pay any attention to me at all. It was as if I was invisible to them or simply didn't matter.

"Why am I down here this time Midnight? What do you want from me?" I inquired.

"I'm not the one who decides where you sit in this place Malachai, you are. What do you see when you look around where you're sitting?" Midnight asked, still not revealing himself.

"I see a lot of filth and garbage from other people's desires and pleasures. But I don't take part in any of these things." I answered.

Midnight's form slowly took shape as his figure walked down the stairs behind me, stopping just at the bottom close to where I was.

"Do you see how distracted you've become? At one time you would have seen all the people around you and how much they are hurting and suffering. Now you only see the garbage and filth left by them. Then you defend yourself as not taking part with any of it. Now can you see why you're sitting here this time?" He stated.

My heart sank within me. I knew his words were true. I had forgotten everything I knew was right. I was no longer concerned for people's lives, just my own.

"Why don't the server demons pay any attention to me though? Do I no longer offer any kind of threat? Am I simply not important enough any more for them to even bother with?" I asked.

"They know better than to offer you anything. If they actually paid some attention to you directly, you might remember what you're supposed to be fighting. So if they leave you alone and pretend you're invisible, then you won't bother with them either. So far it seems to be working too. After all Malachai, you are more concerned with what's around you now, than who." Midnight answered.

Immediately the wooden floor in the center of the room began to cave in and break apart, and then it started falling into the flames underneath. Several people standing where the floor was fell below too and I could hear their screams of pain from the fiery furnace they were in.

I jumped from my seat to go save those close to the edge, pushing my way through the crowd of people and past the demonic servants blocking my path. As I drew close to the burning hole, I saw a person's hand clawing from inside, trying to pull their way back up. I quickly grabbed their hand, secured my feet and pulled with all my strength.

As I dragged their body back up to more solid flooring, I could feel how hot their arms were from the flames they were almost consumed by. They were alive and safe at least for now.

The person looked up to thank me and I saw their face. It was someone I knew, someone very close to me.

My ears grew silent to all the noise happening around me. I sat in shock that someone I cared about almost fell into the fire. All I could hear was Midnight's voice speak.

"Sitting on the sidelines won't save anyone. Wishing someone else will fight this war won't save them either. Making sure your life is secure and taken care of won't stop what is happening. Only choosing to fight this war and doing what you should be will matter. If you want to save these people, fight with me Malachai. It's the only way to win this war." Midnight finished, and then faded away into a misty fog.

I sat there as everything around slowly faded away as well. I could still feel the heat on my body from the flames, but the sights and sounds were fading away into darkness.

I woke up in my room with a deep sense of sorrow and despair. I knew what the dream meant, but felt a strong disappointment with myself for letting the demons make me forget my purpose and the war.

As I got up from my bed to get a drink from the kitchen, I heard one last voice speak.

"Fight with me Malachai and we can stop those who want to hurt you and your loved ones."

I fell to the floor, put my head on my knees and began to cry. Then I prayed asking God to help me once more.

Chapter 9

For the next few weeks the dream stayed heavy upon my heart and mind. The dream impacted me deeply. I spent a lot of time thinking about my recent actions, the lives of people around me, and what my purpose in life and with God really was. I also couldn't get over the thought that Midnight was the one teaching me this lesson. Every time I think I know who he is and what he is, something changes that makes me question it all. Is he an angel, a demon or something else?

My life always seemed so busy and cluttered with problems, mostly caused by my need to help and care for others. However, whenever I tried to spend even a little time to get my own life figured out, everything else around me seemed to fall apart. It just didn't seem fair.

I needed a break and time to myself, so I decided it was time to take one. There was a quiet place, just a short drive from where I lived, that I used to go to for some solitude. Lucy and I often went there when we just needed to get away and talk by ourselves. I decided this was exactly what I needed.

My place of solitude was past all the houses and farms, then just a short drive down a gravel road that bordered on a large river. The trees were just starting to come alive after their winter rest and the buds were just beginning to open and reveal the fresh green leaves inside. There was a refreshing breeze blowing along the river causing the trees to gently sway around me. Even the river seemed calmer today and flowing briskly along without a care in the world. As I looked around I could see many birds enjoying the breeze and singing their songs of joy. Above me were a couple eagles soaring in their circling patterns looking for fish in the river below.

Everything was calm and I was beginning to feel relaxed once more. I sat down along the edge of the river with my bible in my hand and began simply talk with God and listen for His answers.

After a while I leaned back against a tree to enjoy the calmness of the moment when I noticed how quiet everything had become. The birds were no longer singing; the trees had become calm and even the river seemed quieter. But, I could faintly feel the presence of someone nearby.

"Whose here? Can I help you? I know you're there." I spoke loudly.

But there was no answer, just the feeling of someone watching me.

Again I spoke, even louder this time.

"What do you want? You might as well come out; I know you're watching me." I stated.

The feeling of someone nearby grew stronger and the image of an older, dark, shadowy man began to appear on the one side of me, drawing closer to where I sat. I knew it wasn't Midnight; this spirit was shorter and gave off a very different sense. I wasn't sure whether to stand up, run or just sit and wait to see what this spirit wanted. So I leaned forward with my hands and feet at the ready, in order to prepare for doing all three choices.

Then I addressed the spirit.

"Who are you and what exactly do you want with me? Do you intend any harm?" I asked.

The spirit came to within a few feet of me, allowing me to see his darkened eyes, revealing he was definitely a demon. Then he stopped and answered.

"My name is not important. What I am you already know. I'm not permitted to harm you or else I already would have. So the only question left, is what I want. I wish to talk with you but I had to make sure no one else was watching first." The spirit said.

I looked around us, and then asked, "Who else was watching?"

"With you Malachai, there's almost always someone watching. However, your time of prayer with God has caused any of my kind who are not comfortable around His presence, to leave temporarily. But they will be back." He replied.

"So you're not uncomfortable by God's presence?" I questioned.

"I didn't say I wasn't. I'm just desiring time alone with you more than my comfort." He stated.

I looked carefully into his eyes to see deeper within his soul and knew he was sincere with all he was speaking.

"Well if our time is short, then please go ahead and ask whatever it is you need to know." I said.

He came a little closer, then sat on the ground beside me and positioned himself to face me.

"I have watched you from afar. I have listened to your words to others. I know how Midnight favors you and how God watches over you. I know you understand much about my kind and how our choices led to our own fall and eventual punishment, just like your kind's sins did. However, I have heard you praying for my kind before, asking God to help us and bring us hope too. Do you mean it? Do you actually believe there is hope for us too?" The demon questioned.

I could feel his deep sorrow, almost regret for his actions.

"Yes, I do. What Jesus did on the cross was for everyone in heaven and on earth that choose to believe. The bible says that all things in heaven and earth are put under Jesus' authority. I do believe that includes your kind too. That's why I have authority over you; it's because of Jesus and my choice to believe in His way, not because I have any real power. So if Jesus' authority can be used to control you, then I believe His forgiveness can be used to help you too. You just have to accept Jesus' authority over your life and start doing things His way, rather than your own. Do you honestly believe you can surrender yourself completely like that after being in control of your own destiny for so long?" I responded.

"Now there's something to laugh at. Do you honestly believe we have control over our own destiny? We are subject to as many rules and rulers as you are, maybe more. That's why the idea of surrendering to Jesus makes so little sense. It seems like just letting another ruler command you. There really is no freedom for anything God created. Have you not figured that out yet? Freewill and choice are guided by the situations, circumstances and consequences around us all. None of us get to do what we really want because the consequences cause us to choose actions that consider the outcome in one way or another. Therefore even with Jesus we are not really free." The spirit shared.

I took a moment to think and silently pray, asking God for wisdom.

"I guess the ultimate choice comes down to a person's interpretation of freedom. If freedom is serving under someone who is more concerned about their own control and well-being, so I can do the same as long as I don't disobey their rules or affect their well-being, then I guess to some it's freedom. However, if freedom is serving under someone who sees a bigger purpose beyond my immediate existence that allows me to use my personal abilities and gifts to have a part in that existence to benefit myself and others, then perhaps it's a not such a bad freedom to accept." I answered.

Then I turned to face him directly and continued.

"Like you said, we are all basically following someone else's rules in one way or another; there is no real free-will except to choose which set of rules. However, if you honestly think about it, the choice God gave us was not a rule free existence, but the knowledge of good and evil. Both have rules and many want to control how those rules are interpreted. But to me it makes sense to allow the one who understands every aspect of those rules to help and guide my life to encourage the best possible existence for me and others." I finished.

"I can see why Midnight likes you. Your words have wisdom in them, which can even cause my kind to consider our ways. So, I can choose to serve the Christ and regain my place under God's control. Or, I can continue serving my own ways and fall subject to every ruler who places themselves in greater positions than mine. Do you believe God will take me back?" The spirit asked.

"Yes, why wouldn't He. God created all things and He loves all He creates. You of all His creations should know that His desire is to have a relationship with us built on trust and love. You just have to get beyond your own self-centered opinions and see things from His point of view. He loves all of us and desires all of us to be with Him, but it's our choice as to which rules we follow." I answered.

"I do miss Him and serving under His ways. Somehow they always had the greater purpose you are talking about. When the anger fades and pleasures no longer satisfy; you begin to think about why you made those decisions you did. Even though my existence has been to influence your kind's choices, there comes a time when even some of us consider why we exist and do what we do. We all serve someone, the choice is just deciding who." He shared.

The winds began to pick up abruptly along the river, blowing directly towards us. The waves on the top of the water grew more intense and the trees began to bend more and more from the vigor of the winds.

"I have to go now Malachai. They are returning and I'm sure they've already seen me talking with you. They will want to know what you said and why I stayed." He spoke.

"Tell them I commanded you to stay and listen. I can do it right now if you want." I said.

"I'll be alright Malachai. You've given me much to consider and I thank you for answering me. If you are right, I may not have to worry about what they think for much longer anyways. Perhaps we will meet again someday. In the meantime be careful, they are always watching you and waiting for any chance to get you under their control. Don't let them win." He finished.

The moment the spirit said his last word, a gust of wind blew across us causing his image to break up like a cloud of dust, and he was gone.

The winds continued blowing strongly around me for another few minutes, then everything settled down and I could hear the birds singing once more.

I used to speak to the angels and demons when I was younger about the things of God, but it all seemed so long ago now. Perhaps this demon was one of those I used to talk with back then.

The thought of Jesus' forgiveness being for everyone seems so simple to me. It just surprised me that these beings created before us and seeing so much more of God's power and purpose would question His love and forgiveness for them too.

I guess they have more in common with us than they might like to think; they choose to make God's purposes much more complicated than they are, just like we do.

When I arrived back at my apartment, I began to search my pocket for my keys to the main entrance of the apartment building. While I stood there before the doors searching my jacket, another man I didn't recognize came up beside me. He was middle aged and well dressed in a very fancy suit and tie. He pulled out his set of keys and began unlocking the main door.

"Here, I'll get the door for you. I know you live here; I've seen you around a few times." The well-dressed man said.

I stopped looking for my keys, turned to the man and said, "Thanks, I appreciate it. I'm not sure where I put my keys; they're usually in my one pocket."

Once the man opened the door, he held it for me while I went past and entered the building. Suddenly a feeling of terror shot through my soul and I quickly turned to face the man.

"You crossed the line this time Malachai. You interfered with our ways for the last time. We know everything about you, but you know much less about us than you think. Your Christ is not for us and His teachings should not be spoken to our kind. You obviously are not learning to keep out of our business. But you will soon." The well-dressed man spoke in a very harsh tone with a demonic, angry look on his face.

I stood there for a brief moment, stunned and scared.

"I have to do what is right. Just remember I serve God and if you try to hurt me you will have to deal with Him and His angels too." I spoke, nervously.

The feeling of terror left as quickly as it came and the well-dressed man's face had turned back to normal. He was now just looking at me confused and a little nervous.

"What are you talking about? I'm not going to hurt you; I'm just holding the door so you can get in the apartment." The man said.

I took a moment to compose myself; then answered.

"Uhmm, I'm sorry. I thought you said something else to me, but I guess I'm just hearing things. It's been a long day. Sorry." I replied.

He quickly walked past me and headed towards the elevator.

"It's okay, but perhaps you need to take a break and get some rest." He said, still acting nervous.

"Yah, that's a good idea. Sorry again." I answered.

As the well-dressed man got into the elevator, I stood in the apartment lobby for a moment to ponder what just happened. Did it all really happen or was it just my imagination? Or was the man momentarily consumed by a demon that was honestly threatening me?

I decided to take the stairs to my apartment and not take any chance of being in a confined space at the moment, like the elevator. When I came to the door of my apartment, I reached into my pocket once more for my keys and this time they were right where I had always put them, in same jacket pocket I had searched before.

I knew it had to be a demon then within the well-dressed man. The problem was what to do now. I was definitely scared by what he said. Maybe I did cross the line by ministering to the demon at the river. But I had to do what is right; and leading people or spirits towards God's purposes is what is right.

"So if I did what is right, then why do I feel so afraid right now God?" I spoke out loud, as I entered my apartment.

I spent the rest of the night praying, reading the bible and checking around the apartment continually to make sure I was alone and safe. All I could do was trust God to watch over me now.

Chapter 10

As the days and weeks went on I began to understand what the demons real threat was all about. When he approached me at my apartment I thought he might physically attack me, now I realize the attack was meant to cause me grief and despair.

Over the past few weeks I was hit with one financial problem after the next. With extra car repairs, increases in apartment expenses, extra demands at work wanting me to choose my priorities of jobs and even jealousy from co-workers; I felt busier than ever. I knew I couldn't keep the pace up and had to make changes, but I really didn't want to give up the apartment. I just couldn't afford it on my own anymore.

On top of my own problems, it seemed like many of my friends and family were struggling with all sorts of strange issues and problems. Even neighbors in my apartment were experiencing weird problems with their apartments, cars and lives. I began thinking everything that was happening to them was my fault and did my best to pray for them all, trying hard to command any spirit attacking them to back off. However, each time one person's life settled down, another person began having a real rough time.

I was feeling exhausted mentally, physically and spiritually. Even Lucy couldn't seem to cheer me up anymore. I was being dragged back down once more into the pit of despair and desperately needed help.

That night I had another dream; one that was revealing itself in pieces over the past several weeks. Each time I dreamt it I would see and feel more of what was really happening. But I never saw the end because I would wake up too soon, until now.

I found myself descending from the clouds to the dirt ground before a large layered maze of walls. On my way down I could see a large battle happening in the center of the maze. People were fighting hard against a horde of beasts and demons. I could see the people swinging their weapons and swords but having very little effect on the enemies they were fighting.

The beasts and demons were also swinging their swords, shooting arrows and even catapulting stones at all the people. Many of the people were being knocked to the ground and slain, as the beasts kept moving towards them.

As my feet touched the ground I could hear the cries of those in the center of the maze and knew I had to get there quickly to help. However, each layer of walls only had one doorway in order to get through; and there were different hazards or people blocking each door.

The first door was always hard to see as it was hidden behind many small shrubs and vines. Most of the plants were covered in thorns and thistles destined to snare my clothes and skin, ripping as I passed through. Somehow I would always find a strong stick lying nearby to help break through the brush, but I had to take the time to look for it.

Just as I would make it to the door itself, a person would appear to speak the same message to me. The person would change each time and was always someone I sort of knew, but the message was the same.

"Is it really your fight to be involved with Malachai? Stay out of here and you will be safe. If you choose to enter this door you will put yourself into this war and the consequences will also be yours." The messenger would speak.

"I have to go forward, it's what God requires of me and I serve His purposes, not my own. I must do what is right." Would be my response.

When I entered through the door I found myself in the middle of a barren land. It looked as if a war had happened long ago and every living thing was now dried up and withered away. I could see old riverbeds, dead stumps and logs, even the dried half buried bones sticking out of the dusty ground.

The air was humid and difficult to breath and I would always sweat from the heat coming from the ground. However, I was always cold inside; even my skin was cold to the touch as if death was within me. Whenever I would try to move forward the winds would stir up blowing dust and dirt into my face, filling my lungs.

I would do my best to push forward towards the wall that seemed far off in the distance and hard to see because of the blowing dust. Within minutes of entering the expanse I would have abrasions on my arms as I tried to protect my face from the constant dust scraping like sand paper across my skin.

I could also see several broken down buildings and dugouts cropping out from the ground and scattered through the area. However, for me to use any of the partial shelters I would have to leave the main path that took me to the doorway itself. I knew they were just a temptation though to offer me protection from my suffering, and to be a distraction from the real purpose I was here for. As much as I wanted to go, I knew I couldn't leave the path before me, it wasn't right.

As I finally made it close to the door another person would appear with another message. This person was always one of my close friends, someone who knew me well. Like before, the person would change, but the message was always similar. The message only changed slightly to reflect the messenger's relationship with me.

"Malachai, why are you making yourself suffer so much? Everyone knows how much you care and we all appreciate what you do. But look at your face, hands and arms. Are the scars and pain really worth it? Let me help you. I can take you somewhere safe where you can heal and rest." My friend would say.

I always answered the same though.

"I can't quit now. There are those who need help inside and someone has to try. I can't stop until I have finished what God has purposed for me. It just isn't right." I replied.

Immediately after, I would be standing before the door with my friend still standing beside me. The door handle was a smoldering red and I could feel the heat coming from the door itself from several feet back. I knew whatever was behind this door was even hotter than the barren land I was currently in. Perhaps hell itself was waiting before me.

"Well, go ahead and enter then. Grab the handle and burn yourself. It's what you want isn't it? Don't you believe you need to suffer and take on our pain in order to be a hero, to be like Jesus?" My friend would say.

"No I don't. But if I choose to put my own comfort and safety first while those around me are being hurt or destroyed, how can I say I am a Christian, when I'm not following what Jesus taught and His example? I have to do what's right even if it hurts me because Jesus did what is right even though they crucified Him." I answered.

Then I would take hold of the burning hot door handle, feeling a moment of searing pain burst through my body. I could even hear my skin sizzling like frying meat and smell my own flesh burning, as I turned the handle and entered the next room.

As soon as I walked through the door, my mom, several family members and some close friends quickly came to greet me; crowding around to see if I was okay.

"Malachai, what happened to you? Look at your arms and your hand is severely burned. You need to sit down and get these wounds looked at. Your brothers will get you something to drink and eat. Then you'll feel better." My mom said, while guiding me to a table on one side of the room.

This was only the second time I had dreamt this part of the dream, but I knew what this room reminded me of. It looked like the old wooden saloon from my dreams with Midnight. However, this room was much bigger with less people and there were no demons waiting to serve me, just my family and friends.

The last time I dreamt I was here, I listened to my mom and sat down at the table while her and my brothers dressed my wounds and convinced me to stay with them.

"Why do you have to get so involved with everyone else's problems Malachai? Look how wounded you already are, what good will you be to anyone if you don't take some time to rest and heal. The war will always be happening; you are allowed to take a break." She said.

Last time I listened and decided to sit for just a moment. However, as soon as I made the decision, their appearances changed and they began to strap my arms and legs to the chair with the bandages meant to help me. Then they continued on with their own lives, doing whatever they wanted and left me out of the way, tied to the chair in the corner.

This time, I knew better than to fall for that temptation. So I pulled my burnt hand away from my mom and began walking directly to the door on the other side of the room.

My brothers both stood in my way, while several other family members and friends gathered towards me.

"You can't help them, who do you think you are anyways, Jesus. Everyone has the right to make their own choices and you should just let them live with their consequences. Look at you, if don't start living a little and enjoying your life, you're going to die miserable. Maybe God is trying to help you understand that life is for the living, so you need to quit taking it so serious and start doing what makes you happy and feel good." My brothers said, both taking turns speaking.

"If I simply do what everyone else does, then you're right I might be happier for now. But, how long will getting what I want last when it starts to encroach on you getting what you want. If I should be more concerned with myself before thinking of others, what happens to your freedoms when they interfere with what I want to do? Isn't that how wars are started? But if you all cared more about those who are hurting and suffering rather than your own comfort, we could work together and end this war completely." I answered, while pushing past them all.

"You'll lose though and they'll kill you just like they did your Christ. But you're not God, so you can't come back from the dead. What good will you have accomplished then?" One of my brothers stated.

"I have to do what God wants, not what I want. Even if I die, I have to do what's right." I replied.

They all continued speaking over top of each other trying to tell me how wrong I was for continuing. However, as I arrived at the door and began to reach for the door handle I heard another voice speak.

"Please don't continue Malachai. I need you and don't want you to get hurt. If you go through that door you will be leaving me behind too." Lucy spoke.

I put my hand down and turned to see her standing beside me with tears rolling down her cheek. As I reached up with my burned hand to wipe her tears, I watched in amazement as her tears ran into my burns and began to heal them. Within moments the wound was healed and just a scar remained. I didn't want to go forward anymore, I just wanted to stay with her, but I knew it wasn't right.

"I love you Lucy, and I hope you will understand why I must go forward. I have to go through this door because I have to trust God's purpose more than what I might want to do. If I don't do what I know is right, you will lose me anyways, because I will stop being who God created me to be. Like so many others in this room, I will be stuck, lost and tied down forever. Please trust God Lucy." I said.

"I guess God is even more important to you than I am. So I hope you can find some happiness with Him, because I'm obviously not enough for you. Look what He's put you through already, all your scars. Even after I healed you with the love in my tears, you still don't want me." Lucy stated; then walked away to join the rest of the people.

I desperately wanted to chase after her, but I knew it wasn't right. I had to keep going forward. So I turned the handle and entered into the next room.

There was complete darkness here. The room was empty of all light, sound and feeling. Just empty. I quickly tried to find my way through the room but I had no idea where I was going. Even the door I came through was gone and I felt completely alone.

I spent what felt like hours in the place trying desperately to find any type of structure other than the floor. I tried jumping up hoping to find a ceiling. I even crawled along the floor hoping to find something small that I might be missing. When I yelled out, my voice simply vanished in a deep dark abyss. I felt alone and began to feel afraid.

After what seemed like hours of being lost in the darkness, I started questioning why I started this journey. The words everyone else spoke to me ran through my head and I questioned if I was wrong all along. I began doubting who I was and why I thought I was good enough to fight this war in the first place. Then I started getting angry with God for making me the way I was and for causing me to follow His purpose in the first place. So I fell to the ground, with tears flowing down my face and cried out to God.

"Why did you bring me this far only to abandon me here in this place God? Why? I've always felt so alone and that no one understands why I feel such a need to serve you. But I do it anyways. Even when they judge and criticize me I do what is right. But you always leave me alone to be hurt and condemned. Maybe I'm just not good enough for what you want, maybe you just chose the wrong person to fight this war. I don't even understand what the war really is anyway. I'm just tired of living in this darkness God. Please, if You care at all, help me. I need You; I need Your light to guide me before I'm lost in this darkness forever." I spoke out loud, desperately hoping that God could still hear me.

When I finished a dim light began to shine. It wasn't coming from somewhere else in the room; it was coming from within me. Every scar and wound on my body was shining as well and the brightness grew the more I stood back up and focused on the light.

"When you feel like you are alone Malachai, it is because you have forgotten my promises. I said I would never leave you, nor forsake you. I am with you always because you chose to believe in me and follow my ways. You just became too focused on the darkness and covered My light which I placed within you. You are my light to others when you do what is right Malachai. But you have to choose to believe in who I know you are and trust in My help to guide you. Avoiding all the distractions of the world is not easy, but if you trust Me, I will be with you always." The voice of the Lord spoke.

"I trust you God. Please guide me forward once more. I'm willing to listen and trust you." I answered.

The light within and around me grew as bright as the day and I could clearly see the entire room finally. It was rather small and the door was easy to find now that there was light to show me the right way.

"Thank you God, I'm sorry for doubting." I said, then walked quickly to the door and opened it up ready to face whatever might be on the other side.

The battlefield lay before me. The sound of screaming and smell of death overwhelmed my senses as I walked through the door. To my right were cages filled with prisoners piled one on top of the other. The people were desperately climbing over each other trying to find a way out of their jail. But there was no opening to escape.

To my left I saw people urgently trying to climb the wall itself, standing and jumping on those who had fallen, almost using them as step stools in order to scale the wall. But the wall was too high and wherever the people were piled high enough for a hope of escape, the beasts came along to tear the piles apart.

The beaten and wounded people would try to limp away, but the beasts were too powerful. Many people were already missing limbs, but the beasts would attack again and again.

In the middle of this blood soaked dirt arena was the intense battle between demons, beasts and people of all ages. Bodies were scattered everywhere of the dead and wounded, but no one cared, they just kept fighting to save themselves. I saw them walk over the hundreds of people missing limbs and bleeding on the ground. Some people were trying to get closer to the battle; others were simply trying to get away from it all.

I watched for a moment trying to figure out how I could help and saw how the demons were even using people to fight others. They promised not to harm them if the person would fight for the demon, and the people listened. I saw some desperately trying to fight back but they would quickly become surrounded and defeated. It all seemed so hopeless, like the war was already won.

Then I heard my name called.

"Malachai, please help me. I'm hurt; you've got to get me out of here." It was one of my friends from the barren room. He was lying on the ground not far from me. His leg was missing and there were wounds all over his body.

I quickly ran towards him to see how I could help, and noticed others I knew. In fact, everyone I knew and everyone I had passed in the rooms were there, including Lucy. She was locked in one of the cages and was now screaming for my help too. There was no way I could help all these people on my own, there were just too many.

I remembered the lessons I had just learned and decided I needed help so I should pray.

"Please God, these are your people. I just can't do this on my own. Help us all, we need you." I prayed.

My prayer was obviously heard, but not just by God. The beasts all took note of me and began coming towards me, ready for battle. Many of the demons pushed aside those they were fighting and raised their weapons to prepare to fight me. Even the people some of the demons were controlling were forced to come to attach me.

"God I need your protection now. You said I'm not alone, ever, so please reveal yourself now and help me." I desperately prayed, while standing firm in my place.

The light began to shine from within me once more, but this time it was even brighter. It became so bright the beasts and demons could no longer see where they were going. So they began slashing their weapons carelessly around them, hitting one another. As they began to wound one another they became angry and fought against themselves, until one powerful demon cried out in a loud voice.

"Stop fighting each other, he is the enemy we seek. We must slay him and the rest will fall." He said, while pointing in my direction.

They stopped fighting each other and began to shield themselves from the brightness coming from within me. They had one purpose, to destroy me.

"This is my servant and I am with him. You will not harm him." Came a thundering voice that filled the entire area around us.

All the demons and beasts fell to the ground for a moment in fear. Then began to get up and retreat towards the wall opposite from me.

"Thank you for helping me and never leaving me alone." I prayed.

As I reached out to help a couple of the wounded people around me, the brightness coming from within me flowed into them and they were healed instantly. I knew I had to get to Lucy as quickly as possible, but there were so many people needing help on the way. So, I turned to those who were healed and gave them instructions.

"God has healed you and if you will believe in His ways, His light will help you heal others too. Please, ask God to help you so you can help others." I said.

Several people began to pray to God and immediately afterwards they began to shine brightly like me. As they healed others, they passed on what I said and more began to shine and more were healed.

I realized why I needed to endure all the rooms now. It took everything I went through to understand true darkness, so now I could appreciate and understand the true light in order to share it with others.

The arena began to fade and dream ended. I was lying in my bed at the apartment once more. My mind was overwhelmed with all I had dreamt, but my spirit was at peace knowing I finally understood its meaning and it was complete.

Chapter 11

The dream seemed to be the final draw for me. I knew I had to make some tough choices about the direction in my life, but how much was I willing to give up. I was spending so much of my time working just to pay my expenses that I no longer had any time to help others and do what I knew God desired from me.

But before making any rash decisions I knew I needed to talk it over with someone I trusted and who cared about my future as well, namely, Lucy. So I invited her over and shared everything with her, my dreams, the demonic encounters, my expenses and even my fears for the future.

"I know God has something bigger planned for me Lucy, but I just don't know what. It's like there is some dim light way off in the distance that's constantly drawing me towards it and I just have to keep moving forward to reach it. I know it's something special and all the answers I'm desperately looking for are there with it. But, no matter how far I travel towards it, the light always seems too far away." I shared.

Lucy held my hand in hers, and then asked, "Did you ever question if part of the problem might be that God needs you to go elsewhere to follow His path for your life. You often feel like you should be a missionary or pastor or something like that; and you often complain about feeling stuck here and know you should be somewhere else. Maybe you need to take this opportunity and go where God leads."

"But what about us though? You do realize it would mean leaving you too. Unless you're ready to give up everything to come with me?" I responded back quickly.

"I don't know for sure what I would do yet Malachai. But I do know you're not happy here anymore and I don't want to be the reason you aren't doing what you know is right. Maybe you're meant to be some great missionary and because you're stuck here, the lives you should be helping are not being helped. It is possible isn't it?" Lucy asked.

I took a moment to think, and deep inside I knew she was right. I wasn't doing what I knew I should be, but I didn't know exactly what I was supposed to be doing. So I just felt so confused all the time.

"I guess anything is possible, but why is it whenever I have had an opportunity to go on a missionary trip, God seems to close the door so I can't go? Everyone tells me I would make a great teacher or pastor, but every time I try to pursue those directions it feels like God blocks the path and directs me another way." I answered.

"He might direct you another way Malachai, but he certainly still gives you the opportunity to teach and pastor everyone you meet. Maybe he just wants you to be a different type of teacher or pastor than what traditional ones are. You've always been a little different anyways, so this could be why." Lucy said, with a grin while snickering quietly.

"Yeah, thanks. I think. But you do make a good point. God did make me a little different and does always seem to teach me in rather strange ways. So what do you think then, should I give up the apartment and maybe some extra work hours so I can pursue whatever God might have for me? Just keep in mind you would be dating a poorer, homeless man who may have to move a long ways away because God takes him there." I inquired.

Lucy began to grin again and gave out a long, "hhmmmmmmm", then asked, "Just how far away do you think God might take you? Can I make any requests?"

"Gee, it's sure great to know you love me so much." I chuckled.

"Of course I love you. I'm just thinking if God took you away to somewhere warm and tropical, then I would definitely come to visit or help out." Lucy said, with a big smile on her face.

"Okay, I guess that's acceptable then. You can ask God to send me to a nice, warm, tropical place; and I'll ask God to make sure you have to be there too. But what about my apartment, do you have any thoughts about that right now? I mean, where would I live? Should I wait until God directs me to somewhere else or should I take a leap of faith and give my notice?" I asked.

"I don't really know what to answer you. You've always been a leap of faith type person, but this is a big leap. Especially when you don't have any clue where you should be and what you should be doing. All I know for sure is you're just not happy with the way things are right now, so you have to do something; but what, I can't say. Have you ever felt like you should be living somewhere else?" Lucy questioned.

"There have been many places I would love to go to, but not many places feel right. In fact only two places really come to mind. I don't want to go to the one now because my mom and brother are living there; and the other is camp." I replied.

"Why don't you want to live by your mom and brother's family? It's only a few hours from here and it's warm, so I would come to visit for sure." Lucy inquired.

"I guess it's a bit of a pride issue. In case you never noticed, I tend to be a little independent and have been for quite a while. I'm used to providing for myself but I also tend to take care of everyone else around me, especially my mom. But living here gave me the opportunity to take care of myself and be separate. I'd also hoped if I stayed away long enough they might actually appreciate everything I did for them before. However, if I move up there everyone will just think I couldn't make it here on my own and I just ran back to be with them to be taken care of. Even though I would find my own place, do my own thing and have my own life, it wouldn't matter, because I moved back with them." I answered.

"Malachai, it doesn't matter what others think, now does it? I would never think any of that because I have been here with you and know what you do for others. What matters most is where God wants you to be; and if God provides for you through your family in order to get you up there to do His will, then you know you should do what is right. Maybe God brought them up there to give you a reason to go. You and I both know that the only way you are ever truly happy is when you doing what is right before God. So, do you feel God wants you up there and that it's His will?" Lucy asked.

"Yes, I have for a while, but I just don't know how to make it happen and what I'm supposed to do once I'm there. I also don't want to leave you Lucy. You know how much I love you; even being a few hours away feels too far." I said.

"Look at the bright side; at least it's a lot closer then some tropical island, right?" Lucy stated.

"Yes, I guess that's true. At least I know I'll have to stay here for the next month for sure, so it gives me a little bit of time to think this all through and seek God's will. I just hope He gives me some pretty clear answers because I don't want moving away from you to be my biggest mistake ever." I shared.

"Don't worry Malachai; I don't think God wants us apart for long either. You would drive Him nuts with your constant praying for Him to bring me to you." Lucy said, again with a big smile on her face.

We continued just talking for a short while longer before Lucy had to head home. At least for now we were still close, which made us both appreciate our time together.

The next night, Lucy and I met with several friends at our favorite coffee place, just to relax and take my mind off my frustrations. I decided to tell them about my decisions to move to another apartment or house, but I wasn't quite ready to say I might move to a different town or maybe even another country, yet.

Ken was one of my closer friends. We had been neighbors for several years when I lived in the townhouse and it was through him that I got the job at the bowling alley when I was younger. Whenever he had the time, Ken would try to join the rest of us for our coffee nights, thankfully tonight he was able to make it.

"Wow, I guess it's a good thing I came out tonight. If you're interested, a friend of my family was just telling us he had a basement suite for rent." Ken said.

"Really, do you know anything about it, like where it is and how much?" I asked.

"I don't know the price, but his house is fairly close to Lucy's, so that will work great for you two. I know he has been doing some renovations on it, so it might not be finished yet, but I can check. He's also a pretty nice guy, so I'm sure he will consider your financial situation when deciding how much to charge for rent too. It wouldn't be as big as your apartment, but it should have enough room for you to be comfortable. If you want, I can take you by the house tomorrow and you can check it out?" Ken offered.

"Yes, that sounds perfect. I'll give you a call after work and we can see what it's like. Thanks so much Ken." I said, excited.

This already seemed like an answer to prayer for me. One day and God is already providing me with a new place to live, which is even closer to Lucy. Perhaps I won't have to move away quite yet and can stay here in the same town.

"I can also check with our apartment building and see if there is something available if you want. There is usually a list, but it doesn't hurt to ask." Darren inquired.

"Absolutely Darren, I would appreciate it. The more leads I can get the better. And, I know God will provide the place that He thinks is right too, but we still have to ask, seek and knock on a few doors." I answered.

"I'll check first thing tomorrow for you then and maybe after you're finished with Ken, you can drop by Theresa's and my place to see what I was able to find out." Darren said.

Darren had been dating Theresa for a while now and they were very much in love. So Darren finally decided to propose to Theresa and now couldn't wait to get married and spend the rest of their lives together. The two of them now lived in an apartment not far from where I currently lived. So Darren and I often met up with each other for bike rides or walks since we were so close.

Theresa and I also became good friends quickly. She had a spiritual sense to her as well, so the two of us could share what we saw and felt about others. Even though her gift was different than mine, it often gave me comfort to be with someone who also understood the spiritual world.

I couldn't help but think how great it would be living in the same apartment building as Darren and Theresa as well. Lucy and I often spent our spare time with them already as couples, so being closer might even encourage Lucy to think a bit more seriously about our future. Whatever happens though, will still ultimately be under God's control, but it sure is nice to have some options already.

The next day after work I picked Ken up and he showed me to his friend's house. From the outside it was an average sized house, but it bordered on a ravine park along the back. The basement suite had its entrance down a few stairs on the side of the house. Ken was right about how close it was to Lucy as well; her place was just a couple minutes' drive from the house.

However, something about the area bothered me. The air held a strong spiritual sense to it. Something had been this way recently or perhaps even lived close by, but what exactly I couldn't tell. I knew Ken's friend believed in God, but I had also learned how much these spirits could influence even those who believed.

So I took a moment to pray quietly to myself, asking for God's direction, wisdom and protection. I knew whatever this spirit was; it didn't live in this house, but very possibly close by. If God wanted me to live here though, then there had to be a reason for it. Maybe God wanted me here to deal with the spirit or even encourage the spirit to leave.

As we walked towards the stairs to the basement suite, I took a long look to my left. The ravine began on the edge of the property, maybe ten feet from the house itself. It sloped downwards for twenty to thirty feet until it reached a small creek below. There were paths forged amongst the tree-covered hills for people to hike throughout it. The ravine acted as a great divide between two neighborhoods, and this house bordered along its edge.

I now knew where the spirit I felt lived, and it was somewhere down in this ravine. But I certainly didn't feel safe anymore.

"Well come on inside and check the place out Malachai. Great to see you again Ken, bring your friend inside." Tim said.

Tim was a very kind looking person and certainly seemed welcoming. After introducing ourselves, Tim immediately began to show me around the place. It was a bit messy and still not quite finished being renovated, but it had a big bedroom, its own kitchen and a decent sized living room for having friends over.

"So what do you think? I'll get it cleaned up by the time you get here, but will it work for you?" Tim asked, almost as if it was already decided for me.

"It's a good size for me and all, but how much do you want for rent? That's kind of the most important issue for me." I inquired.

"You come with good references Malachai. Perhaps if you can help me out with some yard work and with the renovations we can work out a good deal that helps the two of us. I don't need the money so much but I could definitely use some extra help around here, so it might work out perfect for us both. Especially when it comes to redesigning the yard and cleaning it up, I hear you have a few skills in that department." Tim answered.

"Yes, I can definitely help in that area and if you are willing to give me a good deal with rent in exchange for work, it sounds great to me. Do you need an answer today or can I have a couple days to pray and seek God's will for this as well." I asked.

I knew if Tim wouldn't allow me the couple of days to seek God's will, then this house wasn't right for sure. So for me this was a test to see if it was right.

"Sure, take the rest of the week to decide and let me know by the weekend. I'm planning on listing it in the paper soon, but I can understand needing the time to pray and ask God." Tim said.

After talking a few minutes longer, Ken and I left. I liked Tim and the house, but the strong spiritual sense coming from the ravine made me very uncomfortable. I wanted to know what it was, and I knew if I lived in that basement suite, I would definitely find out.

For now I had to get Ken home and then meet up with Darren and Theresa at their place. God had opened up two doors last night so far one was still wide open, now it was time to check on the other.

Darren and Theresa's apartment complex was older but big. There were three main sections with several floors of apartments and an indoor swimming pool with a recreation area, in the middle of the three complexes. Darren and Theresa lived in the section attached directly to the pool. However, as wonderful as the apartment was, I always had a feeling of darkness and oppression come over me when I visited the complex. Theresa could always feel it too.

"Hey Darren, Theresa, so is there any chance of an apartment for rent here?" I asked.

"Sorry, but no luck. I talked with the manager and he said he has a list of people waiting with at least forty names on it. I even tried to tell him how great of a guy you are, but all he did was chuckle. Apparently he knows who you are and as much as he likes you, it just wouldn't be fair to those who have been waiting." Darren answered, with sadness to his face.

"It's alright Darren, I understand. It would have been nice to be close, but God has His reasons. Right? Thanks for trying though." I replied.

"How did it go with the basement suite then?" Theresa asked.

"Actually, the owner is ready for me to rent it right away by the sounds of it. The place should work at least for now and he will reduce the rent in exchange for my help around the place." I said.

"Well, that must be why God closed this door then, because He's already provided the basement suite." Darren stated.

"Yeah, I guess that's right Darren." I answered.

"Something's wrong with it though isn't there? I can tell by the look on your face." Theresa questioned.

"There was a strange spiritual sense around it, actually coming from the ravine beside the house. I can't quite place what is down there, but it is different from the dark feeling we get around this apartment. Remember the creature I told you about in the park? The feeling coming from the ravine is very similar." I responded.

"But how do you feel about Tim and the house?" Darren asked.

"They seem good. I didn't feel anything wrong there, just around the place." I answered.

"So maybe God needs you there to help Tim and protect him. Maybe God's providing this place so you can get rid of whatever is in that ravine, just like what happened with the satanic house." Darren stated.

"I agree with Darren, I think you should take the basement suite and let God guide you to get rid of whatever the creature might be." Theresa added.

"You guys are right. It certainly seems to be the way God works things. First He convinces me that I need to move, and then the next day He provides me with a new place to live that needs some sort of demon removed to help protect the neighborhood. Sounds logical to me." I chuckled.

"Actually it sounds a lot like how your life seems to work Malachai. I'm glad God doesn't love me like He loves you." Darren replied.

I left Darren and Theresa's and met Lucy back at my place. We spent several hours before she had to go home just talking and praying about all that had happened, desperately seeking God's will. In the end, we both felt it was right that I took the basement suite, despite what might be in the ravine. However, I had also decided to wait until the weekend before giving Tim a firm answer, just in case God wanted to provide another option.

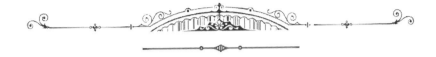

Chapter 12

I had only lived in the basement suite for a week, but already I questioned how long I wanted to stay. Whether it was night or day I always felt like I was being watched. Often I could hear whispers from of voice that didn't want to be heard completely. The words I could understand were designed to cause me to be on guard and afraid. Each time I heard the whispers I prayed and told the spirit to leave, which it always did very quickly.

I knew what this spirit was trying to do, if it could scare me enough then I would leave. So by making its short attacks to cause me to be uncomfortable, then leaving as soon as I began to pray or command it, the spirit could protect itself from fighting a more serious battle.

The problem was that God brought me to this place and had a purpose for me to be there. This meant I had to stay until I had done what God needed me to do. I just wished I knew exactly what I was dealing with. This spirit wasn't like most of the others I had dealt with. It had an initial sense of power to its presence, but the longer it spent around me I could also sense a cowardliness within.

I had just finished my late night shift at work when I arrived back to a darkened house and basement suite. I knew I had left the side house light on, but now it was off. Tim usually left a light on outside as well when he knew I was working late, but every light both inside the house and outside it was now off. The neighbors still had power and the streetlights were still on, so I assumed Tim must have simply forgotten and turned everything off.

I carefully walked down the narrow pathway towards the basement stairs using the bushes and side of the house to help guide me. There was just enough light coming from the streetlight out front of the house to cause a slight glow on the short fence, trees and bushes bordering along the ravine side of the yard, which helped me find my way to the stairs.

However, just as I reached the top of the stairs I heard movement in the bushes just on the other side of the fence from me. I could also feel the eerie dark presence of the spirit there too. It was watching me and I could faintly see the pale orange eyes of some sort of creature staring at me from behind the trees and bushes.

I froze in my place and just waited to see what its intentions were. I certainly didn't want to turn my back to whatever this creature was and give it opportunity to strike me. From the height of its eyes within the trees, it wasn't small and must have been at least seven or eight feet tall. Its spirit was also different from most other demons I had encountered which made me even more curious to know what it really was.

"I know you're there, I can see you. Now I command you through the authority of Jesus the Christ to tell me what you want! Why are you bothering me?" I stated.

The creature shifted its stance within the bushes to move a little closer to the fence and me, while still keeping its figure hidden amidst the trees.

"You're the one intruding here, not me. I was fine before you came here. This is my territory and I keep it perfectly controlled. But you are unwelcome here and are only causing problems by your presence. I want you to leave my territory so I can be at peace." The creature spoke.

"What do you mean, how have I caused any problems? I've lived here less than two weeks and haven't even met you until now." I said.

"It's what follows you that concerns me. Not only does your Christ dwell strong with you, but His enemies follow behind you as well. Now that you are here, they invade my territory to watch you, and they cause havoc within those they encounter, disobeying my rules. My territory may be small, but it is still mine. I can't fight a war with them and they know it. So I need you to leave so I can keep control over those who belong to me here." The creature answered.

"Have you ever considered whether your having control here is right? Perhaps I've been brought here to break your control over this area. Maybe you need to be the one who leaves." I stated.

The creature's spirit became greatly agitated as it moved closer to the side of the fence. I could now see a faint glimpse of its face. It definitely didn't look human but wasn't completely a beast either. It's rough skin was grayish black like smoke and its nose and mouth protruded off the front of its face about half the length of a horse, much like a goat. It was definitely tall but I knew it was still crouched down too as it drew close to speak with me.

"I have ruled here long before you were ever a thought and I have fought many who tried to remove me. My territory was once vast and powerful before the one who covets you came to claim it for his own, and now you want to take the rest from me. You're an arrogant fool who will lose everything because of your beliefs." The creature replied.

"You're talking about Midnight aren't you? He's the one who took the rest of your territory and you think he sent me here to take what's left. But it's not true, I don't serve him, I serve God; and I would never give this territory over to Midnight." I spoke.

"What do you think will happen when I am removed from here, God will simply leave it up to His people to rule? Never! Midnight will bring his kind here and rule it for himself and I will have to find a new area to rule. Your kind are merely pawns in a game which you couldn't possibly understand and God only ensures we don't break the rules. So what benefit will there be for anyone by removing me and allowing Midnight to rule instead? Except you of course, you will gain more favor from him by removing me." The creature stated.

"I will never do his will, nor do I desire his favor. I serve God first, never misunderstand that fact." I replied, angrily.

Immediately an intense heaviness flooded the area and a wind began to blow from the west against me.

"Now you made him angry and it's time for me to leave. Don't drag me into this war Malachai, just leave before things get worse and I am forced to fight you and them." The creature said.

Then it took a few steps back into the trees and I could hear it move quickly down to the bottom of the ravine and it was gone. Once the creature left, the light on the side of the house and in the carport clicked on again and I could see everything clearly. The wind continued to blow briskly around me, so I decided it was best to get down the stairs and inside the house before Midnight showed up as well. For the next several hours I just prayed and read my bible while in my bed because there was no way I wanted to go to sleep after what just happened. However the fatigue eventually got to me and I fell asleep with my bible in my arms.

But my sleep was short as nightmares filled my dreams. I was in a continual fight for the survival of many people, most of whom I didn't know. They were under attack from an army of demons and large dragon like creatures that were trying to control them. Many of the people were being enslaved by the hordes or were severely wounded because they resisted. Yet I seemed almost useless to help the people because the demonic armies were so vast and were attacking much too furiously.

When I woke up from the nightmare, I knew I had to do something, but what? This creature had brought up a couple questions I hadn't thought of before. Was it Midnight who brought me to this place or was it God, and will I be causing a war that will hurt many others by simply staying here. However, the problem was how could I be sure as to who brought me to this basement suite. It all seemed to be a blessing by God up until now.

"God, please I need your guidance now. I certainly don't want to cause the people in this area any problems or put them in a middle of a war because of my presence here. So, I won't do anything against this creature or any demon that is here until you give me some sort of clear sign that it is your will. Otherwise, if it is Midnight trying to use me, please tell me or move me somewhere else so he can't win. I want to do your will only and need you to show me what it is." I prayed.

Then, for the rest of the night I just stayed awake in my bed, reading and talking to God.

The dreams and nightmares just continued though for several weeks and I could feel the presence of the creature watching. It kept a greater distance from me this time and I knew the creature had no intention of being close enough for me to speak to it again. However, I could also sense the spirits of several other demons gathering into the area and it was becoming more obvious that the battle lines were being drawn.

"Would it be so wrong if it was me helping you Malachai?" The voice spoke.

I was dreaming again and was standing in the middle of the foggy field close to my old house. It was the same field with the old wooden shack where Midnight had originally revealed himself to me. I found myself standing among the tall grass, facing the rustic and worn, wooden shed, watching as the door slowly swung open to reveal a black mist now flowing out towards me.

The black mist floated above the grass in the field and slowly moved its way to where I was standing. As it moved it almost enveloped the light in front of me casting a shadow on everything around me. When it drew near the mist began taking the form of a tall dark dressed man with a pale face, and hollow blackened eyes. It was Midnight.

"What do you want now?" I questioned.

"Just to talk with you Malachai. I know about your nightmarish dreams and the war lines being drawn, but it's not me who is causing it all. They're the ones deceiving you and trying to make you fight." Midnight spoke.

"Who exactly are they?" I asked

"Another of God's creations. They are intelligent and very crafty, and do not like anyone invading their domain. They rule their spiritual realm individually as kingdoms and only gather together with their kind to fight foes much too powerful for them on their own, such as your Christ. By you moving into its territory, you have brought your Christ's authority with you; as well as, the demons that keep watch on you and are ruled by more powerful spirits than them." Midnight answered.

"You mean spirits like you? Tell me Midnight, are you the one who opened this door for me, so I could move into the basement suite?" I asked.

"Yes, I am. You were forgetting who you are and what you are supposed to be doing. You were so busy and tired, that you needed help. By bringing you here I've rekindled your fire once more and given you the opportunity to fight for something greater than yourself again." He said.

"So, you've actually done me a great favor then and I guess I should be thanking you right? But I'm sure you've done all this selflessly as well. Getting me to fight this creature and removing it from this area so your troops can quietly take over, probably never crossed your mind. It would simply be a blessing you receive for your act of kindness towards me, right?" I questioned, sarcastically.

"What need do I have for a few city blocks worth of people, my territory is far greater than you realize. This creature is also way beneath my time and trouble. If I wanted this area, I would simply take it and make the creature serve me. You just don't understand how important you are to me, Malachai. When you start forgetting who you are and what your purpose really is, then I must intervene because I need you." He answered.

"You mean you actually did it all to show me my importance and how powerful I can be if I work with you then. But what about God, where is His role in all of this?" I asked.

"Aren't you the one who believes God has the ultimate control over all that happens? He allows us free will, but diligently watches to make sure we don't push that will too far. If God didn't want you to move here and fight this creature, then why hasn't He provided you with an alternative?" Midnight stated, to challenge me.

"Maybe that's a question I need to ask Him then. It is possible God may use you to help me, but it's also possible you might use me to help you. There's more you're not telling me, that I know for sure. So, I guess for now the only way I will find out the real truth is to ask God and let Him reveal what's really going on. At least I'm learning how far you will go to have me on your side." I said.

"You have no idea just how much I can offer you Malachai. This is nothing compared to what I could do to help you. But you simply think too much like a human, only of what is here and now. If you could just open up your mind to what is possible then you might understand what is really going on around us all. At least you are still listening, for now that will have to do." Midnight spoke.

Then, his figure dissipated into the black mist once more and it spread across the entire field, mixing itself amongst the tall grass and disappearing from sight.

I stood there for a moment taking in every sight and sound, and then prayed out loud.

"God I need Midnight's deception undone. Please provide me with an alternative place to live if it is not your will to fight this creature. I need you to reveal what is right and true so I am not deceived." I prayed.

I felt a calm breeze blow across the field and me. Then I woke up in my bed with a ray of sunshine streaming in through a crack in the curtains. Somehow I felt at peace, which was a feeling I hadn't had for a while.

Only a couple of days had past when I received a call from Ben. The camp was booked solid with school groups, church groups and various activities throughout the spring and they were finding themselves a bit short handed. They also needed someone to help clean up the grounds and get it ready for the summer camps.

"Your name came to my mind Malachai, as we were praying and trying to think of who would be the right person to handle all that needs to be done. I know you're working already, but it would be full time and year round work if you are interested." Ben asked.

I could barely constrain my excitement when he asked.

"Yes, I am definitely interested, you know this would be a dream come true for me. Can you give me a couple days to talk to my bosses and make sure it's okay with them? When would you want me to start?" I inquired.

"Of course Malachai, and anytime you are able to start we would love to have you. You can stay with Al the cook, in his cabin and we will even provide your meals. Of course you will be helping to cook and serve them too. You will have to do a little bit of everything, from maintenance to programming; your job will be to help where needed. Don and Mary, the camp caretakers, and I, will let you know what to do once you are able to start. Just let me know when you're ready and the job is yours." Ben said.

"I'll be there as soon as I can Ben. I can't wait; it's an answer to prayer." I stated.

God had answered my prayer and in the best way possible. Not only would I be working at camp, but I would get to live in the one place I felt safe and at peace.

Perhaps Midnight did try to deceive me by getting me to move into this basement suite; or, perhaps God was allowing Midnight to open this door while God was working things out for the camp job. It may also be that God was teaching me how to pay attention to what His will really is and not simply doing what seems on the surface as being right.

Whatever the reasoning was, one thing I knew for sure, I didn't need to fight the creature living in the ravine. God had answered my prayer and provided me an alternative place to be. So staying here and getting involved in the war amongst these spirits was not God's will, just theirs. Instead, God has provided me with a job to serve Him in the one place I truly felt was home.

It took just over two weeks and my move to camp was achieved. Tim wasn't overly happy that I was leaving and my bosses at work were definitely sad to see me go. However, they could all understand why I needed to take the job at the camp and do what I felt was right.

Even Lucy agreed that I had to go. She knew how much camp meant to me and that I needed a place where I felt safe once more and could serve God the way I was meant to. Plus, it was still closer than moving to where my family was, so at least we could still see lots of each other.

As I stepped out of my car and looked around at the camp, I knew this was right. I was finally home.

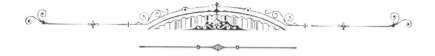

Chapter 13

The first few weeks at my new job passed very quickly. Ben wasn't kidding about how much work needed to be done. The bookings for various groups were almost solid. This meant lots of cooking, cleaning and programs to run. Plus, the general maintenance of the grounds and gardens had to be kept up so those who came could enjoy their entire experience.

My main tasks were to be a Jack of all trades, which meant I was there to do whatever was needed, for whoever needed the help. It gave me continual opportunities to try new things and learn new skills. From cooking for large banquets; using a chainsaw to cut logs; maintaining a hot tub; fixing boats and docks; repairing and testing rifles and bows; preparing arts and crafts; cleaning and gardening; plus, creating activities and programs for schools, churches and groups; I truly believed I had the perfect job.

I may have been very busy all the time, but I finally had the opportunity to use all my skills and abilities to help others and serve God in a place that encouraged me to do so. Plus, the constant challenges and changing tasks gave me the chance to learn more skills and gain the confidence within myself as to what I was actually capable of doing.

Whenever problems began to start at the camp, whether with people who came with one of the groups, neighbors or even equipment, the other five full time staff and myself would get together to pray. As a result, we got to take part in the many miracles and amazing events God was doing through the camp.

Many of the groups that came were not from Christian organizations either, yet they always welcomed our prayers and appreciated how we showed the love of God through our actions and compassion. This then gave us the opportunity to share why we lived our faith differently from others.

Summer had almost arrived and the last school group was just about finished with their week at camp, when the principal, John, asked to speak with me.

"Malachai, I've been a principal for many years and have taken many school classes to camps throughout those years, but I must say this year was the best ever and largely because of you. You are a very different person both with how you treat others and how you share your belief in God. I've watched how everyone seems to listen to what you say and how you listen to all of them, even the most frustrating children. The children we all seem to have the hardest time dealing with are the ones that are almost drawn to you and then they become happier and nicer children just by spending time with you. I'm not sure exactly how you do it, but you definitely have a gift with children that you need to keep using." John said.

I wasn't quite sure what to say. John was paying me a huge compliment and I certainly appreciate that he noticed the extra time I took to help those in need. I also knew he believed in God, but I didn't think he would understand just why I was a little different from others.

"Thank you for the compliment John. I guess I just take the idea of helping those in need a little differently. I've always been a bit of an outsider and misunderstood, so I tend to understand others who are like me. God asks us to love everyone regardless of whether they are likeable or not, so I do my best to show that love and most of the time it seems to work." I replied.

"I guess that is true, we often find it easy to love those who make it easy or are more like ourselves. But being able to love those who make it difficult and don't even love themselves is often hard and most of us simply give up trying. It takes someone special with a unique way of understanding people to continue trying to help a person who doesn't want to be helped anymore." John stated.

"I guess I just see a little deeper into a person than most. I believe everyone wants to be loved and everyone wants help to be something more. But because they've been told they can't or are being forced into a mold that they just don't fit, they lose hope and no longer believe they can be anything more than what their judges say." I answered.

"Like I said before Malachai, it takes someone special to understand these things and obviously you have some experience too." John said.

"Yes, experience in dealing with those feelings definitely does help." I replied.

"However, watching you with the children, teachers and helpers certainly shows you have a real ability for working with people. Every event, game and discussion you planned or took part in went so much smoother and the children loved having you involved. So I have to ask, have you ever thought about becoming a teacher, counselor or maybe even a youth pastor?" John asked.

"I have worked with youth and children for several years here at camp, at church and even worked as a childcare worker for a couple youth. However, as much as I've thought about becoming a teacher, counselor, pastor or something else, I just can't afford it and deep inside I feel God has a different plan for me." I answered.

"Maybe God is training you to be a different kind of teacher, unconventional and outside of the box. Even as a principal I find it difficult to follow the rules all the time, especially when I see those children who don't fit the mold and then fall through the cracks. I try to help where I can, but I'm limited because I have to consider the entire group of children, not just the needs of one. Perhaps you can be the kind of person who helps the one." John said.

I liked what he said and it made complete sense to me in my heart. I was called to collect the lost sheep that wandered away, not to tend to the flock that was safe.

"Thanks John, that actually helps fill in a lot for me. I've always been helping individuals, but just never thought of it as being my purpose. I've often been told I'm wasting my time and should get a real job of sorts, but helping those who don't fit the regular molds of school, church and life is a worthy job to me." I replied.

"See, there you go again Malachai, being different and wise. With all your experience, you could definitely get more job opportunities as a childcare worker or teacher's helper and if you wanted extra training, the courses wouldn't take you long. I know I would hire you at my school based on what I have watched this week. You're good at what you do and someone with your skills is needed not just here at camp but in schools too. Did you ever consider

God might have you here at camp to learn what you're really capable of, so you can do even greater things elsewhere for Him?" John asked.

His words really struck me, especially about learning what I'm really capable of. Midnight was trying to teach me how capable I was with fighting the spiritual realm, now John is telling me how capable I am with helping individual people for God.

Everything John said made sense within my soul and I knew helping the lost, hurting and outcasts is what God wanted me to do. I also knew I was called to fight the spiritual realm that wanted to hurt, destroy and deceive people. However, until now I hadn't considered how much I was already doing both just by seeking God's purpose for my life.

Maybe this is what God was trying to teach me all along, that by doing His will with my choices and actions, I will be capable in everything I do. But, I first had to learn how to listen to what was His will and what was others or my own. Which also meant my time at camp wouldn't last either because I knew deep inside God had another place for me, I just didn't want to accept it yet.

"Could I really get a job working in schools or even doing full time childcare work without having all the proper education?" I asked.

"Yes, there are special circumstances where people who have the experience will be hired even though they don't have a degree. Just because a person has a certificate, doesn't make them qualified to do a job. I would rather hire someone who has a passion and the experience over someone who simply got an education so they could get a job and make money. However, if a person had a passion, experience and education, I would hire them in a second and not let them go." John answered.

"I'll definitely think about it John. If I could get a few courses while working at the same time, then I probably could. However, I guess if God wants me to do it, then I'll have to trust Him to make it all possible too." I said.

"Exactly. And if you ever want to live in the heart of the big city, let me know and I'll find something for you at my school." John finished.

"Thanks, I appreciate the vote of confidence. However, for the moment I think I better get up to the kitchen to help with supper for you guys. I can see Don up by the kitchen giving me the look to hurry up because I'm late." I said, chuckling.

As I left John to get back to work, I felt a sense of hope for my future. John was an important man and he could see something more within me, just like Ben could. He also saw my unique abilities and even though he didn't understand it all, he knew I was capable of much more. It is the thought of what more I could be capable of which excited me the most. Because I knew there was much more waiting for me, I just had to believe it.

The summer had officially arrived and kid's camps had begun. Everything John said was still fresh in my mind and every day I took time to pray, asking God for direction with my life and to watch over the camp. I didn't want to leave the camp because I loved everything about it; however, I knew deep inside this was all just temporary. God had already been showing where I was meant to be, but He was just being patient and preparing me for what was to come.

As the first week of camp came to an end, I was excited and full of confidence with what God had been doing and how He was using me. I took every opportunity He presented to share His love with others and help those in need, including neighbors and even strangers who were at a campsite nearby. The whole area seemed at peace around the camp and people were filled with joy, including me.

I was sitting alone on the porch of my cabin, which overlooked the beauty of the lake. There was a slight breeze blowing towards me, and only a few clouds dotted the deep blue sky. Even the birds where enjoying the beautiful day and sang their songs loudly.

I began thanking God out loud for all He has done, and even began praying for all the people living and staying around the lake. However, as I was praying a heaviness began to fill the air and the wind blew stronger.

I stood up against the railing on the porch to get a good look around to see if Midnight or some other spirit was there. Then the wind grew even stronger, blowing hard against the trees around the little cabin. One branch fell of the tree beside me, hitting the railing within inches from me, and then fell to the ground below.

I jumped backwards to avoid being hit and noticed an odd cloud formation growing in the sky over the lake not far from the cabin. As the wind grew stronger, the cloud formation grew larger and darker. The back portion of the cloud seemed to stay where it was, but the front facing me was almost exploding directly at me.

My spirit began to feel overwhelmed with the sense of anger and darkness. Part of me wanted to run inside the cabin, but my curiosity wanted to know what this was. So I stayed close to the door, just in case and began to pray out loud for God's help.

Whatever was in this cloud seemed to hear my prayers and began to take a more distinct form. An enormous head shaped like that of a dragon's took shape within the exploding portion of the dark cloud. I could see its nose, mouth, teeth and hollowed eyes take form and as it grew increasingly closer to me.

The air filled with anger and the entire area became consumed by the shadow of this creature's darkness.

"I have endured you long enough, now I want you to leave my territory before you cause any permanent damage." Came a thunderous voice from within the cloud.

"Who are you? Whom do you serve?" I asked.

"I serve no one! I am the master of this region! You are unwelcome here. NOW LEAVE!" The voice thundered.

By this point the front of the cloud had taken the full form of a dragon with its teeth partially opened to show its power. I knew this creature was very powerful, but I didn't understand what I had done to upset it.

"Why do you want me to leave? What have I done to you?" I questioned.

"I now know who you are Malachai and what you are capable of. I know who follows you and who watches over you. I also know how God favors you. You bring change and upset the order of things. This has already begun to start and I will not tolerate you anymore. Because you see truth, you are dangerous. If you stay I will fight everything you do. If you leave, I will leave this place you love alone." The voice finished.

"I will leave, but only when God directs me to and not sooner. Now I command you through the authority of Jesus to leave this camp and me alone." I spoke, boldly.

Immediately, the force of the winds grew so strong I was almost knocked to the ground. Several more branches broke from the surrounding trees and fell around me. Then the image of the dragon flowed quickly towards me with its teeth opening as it came closer, almost ready to devour me where I stood. However, as it came close to the cabin it turned to the right of the camp property, flying just above the tree line into the mountains beside me and then disappeared completely.

The winds began to settle down instantly and the remains of the cloud dissipated into the air until there was nothing left.

I fell down into the chair on the porch in relief and just took a moment to think and thank God for protecting me. However, the moment was interrupted when Al, the cook who I shared the cabin with, came running down to make sure the cabin was okay.

"Malachai, is everything alright? That was an incredible windstorm that just hit. I could see the trees swaying and branches falling, through the windows in the dining hall. I thought for sure there would be some damage to the cabin from it all." Al said.

I took a couple seconds to compose myself before answering.

"Some of the branches hit the porch, but thankfully none caused any damage." I answered.

"Thank God. But what a strange storm, it only seemed to hit down here. I didn't notice the winds anywhere else other than down here by the water. Do you think it was a spiritual wind? I hope it didn't bring anything that will cause trouble for us." Al spoke.

I decided to confide in Al, even if it made me sound crazy. But I needed to tell someone and could certainly use the prayer right now as well.

"It was definitely something spiritual Al, and if you promise not to judge me too quickly, I'll tell you what happened. And, I could really use your prayers afterwards as well." I said.

Al listened carefully as I told him what happened and afterwards he admitted he'd also experienced strange events before, not quite like this, but still strange. Then we spent a while in prayer asking God to protect us, the camp and even the area from whatever this creature was. Afterwards, we both just sat quietly on the porch listening to the singing from the birds and sounds from waves on the lake.

Finally, after a short time we decided to leave the matter in God's hands. Besides, it was time for us to get back to work and head up to the dining hall to make supper for the few staff members remaining at the camp over the weekend.

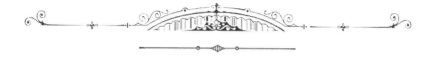

Chapter 14

The next several weeks passed quickly and I finally had a few days off to go visit Lucy and my other friends. However, even after being away for just a day I missed the feeling of hope I found at camp and couldn't wait to get back there.

As happy as I was to see Lucy and my friends, the darkness and demonic oppression I saw everywhere seemed so much more evident than before, and it was depressing. Camp was like an Oasis from the darkness as the light of God seemed to always flood the camp and I felt recharged from it. But here in the real world people don't want God to work His will the same, so darkness rules instead.

As my time off came to an end I felt a change in the air and could feel it in the winds, almost as if a spiritual war was about to begin. Even my friends could feel something different, but none of us could figure out what it was.

When I arrived back at camp the same feeling of an impending attack was here too. The sense of relief and light I was looking forward to was gone and darkness almost surrounded the camp. Whatever I felt at home was affecting more than just me; even the camp was being attacked. I couldn't see anything specific, but I could feel a sense of heaviness like a shadow of darkness hovering over the entire valley.

Paul had seen me arrive and quickly came over to welcome me back.

"Malachai, I'm so glad you are going to be here this week, you will definitely be needed. I believe we are in for a very good week and that God has great plans for us. But I'm asking everyone to meet in the staff room for a time of prayer first, because I can sense an attack coming and if we don't commit ourselves and all our plans to God right at the beginning then the enemy will cause a lot of problems." Paul spoke.

"I certainly agree. I can feel it too. But I can't wait to see what God does through us this week if we can simply trust Him." I answered.

However, as the week went on, the rain just wouldn't stop and everyone was getting more irritable and on each other's nerves. The campers were arguing with each other and their counselors. The staff was nit picking on everything they could find wrong with the games, meals and campers. Even Paul was getting tired and his nerves were wearing thin with everyone's complaining.

"Are you okay Paul?" I asked.

He looked towards the ground almost to hide his face from me, and then answered. "I know this is all just an attack to distract us all from what God wants to do in the lives of these campers and even us, but it's Thursday already and I think the attack is working. Everyone is just stuck in the cabins hoping the rain will stop and no matter how much we try to tell them about God and His love for them, they only see what's in front of them, the rain. I'm just frustrated that when we feel a little discomfort or go through a situation we don't like, we lose faith and quit focusing on God's plan."

The two of us were sitting on the steps of the staff sleeping lodge, across from us was the playing field that currently looked like a mud bog from the amount of rain we had. There were even small rivers of water running down the gravel walkway in front of us, flowing quickly down the small hill and towards the lake.

As I pondered all Paul's words I noticed how green the trees were. Even the grass that could be seen between the puddles was greener from all the rain. The gravel on the walkway was wet and shiny, all the dust and dirt had been washed away.

"Maybe God is just trying to get our attention off our comforts so we can notice how much is really going on around us." I said.

Paul looked at me with a very confused face. "I think I am missing something here Malachai. What exactly are you trying to say." He asked.

"If we stop fussing and focusing on ourselves for a moment we might notice how much God is taking care of the world all around us so we can enjoy it. Maybe we should teach the campers how much the grass and trees need this rain to stay healthy and strong so we can run on the fields, swing on the tree branches and even have firewood for the campfires. Besides the rain can be compared to God's word, it can sometimes seem overwhelming and soaks in to our very core, but it always strengthens us and causes us to grow." I chuckled.

Paul smiled and even laughed a little.

"I like that Malachai; I think we will focus our bible study time on this today. Maybe we all just need a little attitude check and need to believe God knows exactly what

He is doing. I think what everyone needs is to go on with our regular routine of camp and make the rain part of it. We simply have to enjoy what God has given us. So we will go ahead with waterfront down at the lake today with water games, then have our special dinner and even plan for a campfire tonight. If you can make sure we have a hot fire burning for us Malachai, I would appreciate it." Paul said, with a smile upon his face once again.

"You got it Paul." I answered.

We both got up off the stairs and began preparing for the afternoon activities, and of course to convince all the staff to find the joy in this rain too.

As our attitudes changed, so did the campers. Bible study, the activities, waterfront and even our special supper all went incredibly well and everyone had a lot of fun. We had given everyone who needed one, garbage bags to wear as raincoats while they walked from place to place and even made hats for anyone who didn't have one. Of course during waterfront many of the campers didn't care about the rain since they wore their bathing suits and played water sports, water balloon toss or simply swam in the lake.

In the matter of a few hours everyone was forgetting about the misery of the rain and finding fun and joy despite it. Perhaps this was God's plan all along, we just needed to be reminded that joy doesn't come from what is happening around us, but from how we choose to find what is good in it. By the sounds of the laughing and horsing around, I think everyone has decided to find the good once more.

However, the biggest hurdle was yet to come, campfire. I had already put whatever semi-dry pieces of wood I could find underneath some plastic, but there wasn't much. The campfire pit itself was also full of water, which could be another problem. Then there were the benches that had been rained on all week and were saturated with water. Paul had given me a bunch of plastic to cover the seats with as campfire began, but this was definitely going to take a miracle to pull off tonight.

I decided to go up to the campfire area early to prepare and pray. I created a drainage trench leading away from the campfire pit to help reduce the puddle that had formed. Then I collected whatever paper and kindling I could find that wasn't completely drenched. Everything felt damp, even the paper I had tightly wrapped up into plastic, felt damp. It was still raining hard too.

"Please God, we need you to help us. We have been praying all day for the rain to stop and I understand if it isn't your will that it stops it's because you have a purpose in it. But if you can even make it slow down so we can have this one campfire this week, we would all be very thankful. If you can even help me with this fire, everything I have is damp and wet, but I know you can make it work anyway, so please cause this fire to burn hot and bright to keep everyone warm so they forget about the rain. Thank you for helping to change our attitudes today as well. I am truly thankful." I prayed.

Immediately, I felt a breeze flow through the area and I felt at peace. So I assembled the damp paper and kindling in the center of the fire pit, struck a match, and lit the paper. The paper was slow to start, but then the light breeze swept across the fire pit and the flames began to grow. The paper and kindling caught fire quickly, so I began added more wood. Within minutes I had a hot campfire burning brightly and fierce with a rainstorm pouring all around it.

Just then Paul called for me from down below the campfire area. I quickly went to him, hoping he wasn't planning on canceling the campfire now after God helped start this awesome fire.

Paul was standing by the edge of the playing field closest to the walkway leading up to the campfire. There were already three other support staff with him, people he knew trusted God and were strong believers in the power of prayer. He had often called the five of us together to pray for people or situations and this was no different.

"I've asked you to meet me here before the campfire so we can pray once more and perhaps God will give us the miracle we seek. The campers will be heading up to the campfire any moment now and Malachai has a nice fire burning too. I believe God wants to do something powerful in the lives of these campers tonight but this rain just isn't stopping. I want to have the campfire as planned, but I can't have the campers getting so wet and cold they get sick. So, I want us to spend some time in prayer once more and seek God's will for what we should do tonight. Let's pray." Paul said, then bowed his head and we each began speaking out to God as our hearts felt lead.

We prayed for several minutes, until we heard the campers start running past us to go up for the campfire. It was still raining but the campers were excited to get a campfire anyways. They could smell it and see its flames burning through the brush and trees surrounding the area, and they couldn't wait to get up there.

"Well we have given this evening to God and will trust His plan for what happens. It's all in His hands, and I personally hope this rain will stop, even for just a little while." Paul said.

Then we all headed up to the campfire.

It continued to rain as we walked up the gravel roadway from the playing field that lead up the hill to the newer cabins and past the path to the campfire. The path leading to the campfire area was dirt and currently a little muddy, but had two big cedar trees marking its entrance to the main campfire area itself. The campfire area had several rows of benches surrounding the campfire pit in a semi-circle to allow a place at the front for the song leaders and speakers to face the campers.

As I walked towards the campfire to add more wood, I noticed how hot and bright it was burning already. I also noticed that no one had taken any of the plastic sheets to cover their benches with. In fact all the benches looked fairly dry. I approached the fire anyways and threw a couple more logs into it, but couldn't feel the rain anymore. I looked back towards the two big cedars marking the entrance and it was still raining there, however, it wasn't raining right here by the campfire itself.

I took a step back towards the entrance, a little stunned yet excited. Paul had already opened the night up in prayer and the worship team had begun singing some fun camp songs. No one else seemed to have notice yet but me. It wasn't raining anymore, well at least not around us.

I walked back towards the entrance and out onto the dirt pathway; out here it was definitely still pouring with rain. But when I went back into the campfire area, passing the two cedar trees, the rain stopped and everything was drying up. As I looked upwards towards the sky I could actually see the stars above us.

Quietly I called Paul to come over to me.

"Paul do you notice anything unusual?" I asked, excitedly.

"Yes, the fire is burning incredible tonight and very warm. God is with us for sure tonight." He answered.

"No, look around us. Look up too." I exclaimed.

Paul began to look around and when he looked towards the sky he understood what I was trying to say.

"We've gotten our miracle. God's stopped the rain and opened up the heavens. Just look at all the stars shining above us!" Paul spoke, excitedly.

I quickly grabbed his arm and brought him towards the two cedars and the dirt pathway.

"Yah, but check this out." I said while pulling him into the rain on the pathway.

"This is amazing, it's raining here but not over the campfire. Thank you God." He gratefully prayed.

Immediately Paul entered back into the campfire area and interrupted the worship team with the news of this miracle. As he and I began to share about the rain stopping, the incredible fire, dry benches and even the stars above us, everyone was amazed. Many got up from their benches to stand in between the dirt path and two cedars, just to see for themselves how the rain was stopping just at the entrance. Others noticed how the rain had stopped in a circle like line all around the back and sides of the campfire as well. Just outside of the area it was raining, but everywhere inside was dry and we could see the stars. It was a true miracle.

Paul shared about having faith in God's plans for our lives and as he spoke it was obvious the Spirit of God was speaking through him. His stories and words seemed to be speaking to each of our very spirits. We knew what he was saying was truth and that night many lives were changed for God.

Several campers decided to accept Jesus gift of forgiveness and salvation. Others decided it was time for them to trust God with more of their will and lives. Even many of the staff made deeper commitments to follow the ways of Jesus and trust God. It was one of the most incredible campfires ever and everyone was changed for the better in some way.

The fire kept burning warm and bright the entire night. Even when I added more damp wood onto the fire, it dried quickly and burned as if it had never been rained on. The glow of the fire was almost magical with the dancing of the flames and the sound of its crackling.

As the campfire came to a close and we all began to leave past the two cedars, the campers took turns hopping a few more times between the campfire area and the muddy dirt path. It was still raining outside the fire area but dry within it and everyone was completely amazed by what God had done.

I walked back towards the field and the lower cabins with several campers, Matt and some other staff. I was still so excited and amazed as I looked back towards the campfire area and saw how incredible this miracle was once more.

"Hey, stop for a moment and look back towards the campfire area, up above it. What do you see?" I asked the group with me.

Matt was the first to answer. "That's incredible; there is a hole, like a circle in the clouds above the campfire pit. You can see the stars right there but rain everywhere else."

"It's only above the campfire pit too, every where else there are clouds." I said.

Several others had now stopped to see the fullness of God's miracle and were all amazed. Paul had come by with the others from our prayer group and stood with us in the pouring rain, looking up towards the circle of stars in the clouds directly above the campfire.

"God has a purpose for everything that happens, but only when we stop complaining long enough to see what He is really doing, will we understand His greatness." Paul shared, with a smile of contentment on his face.

We sent the campers back to their cabins to head off to bed. Then a few of us went back up to the campfire to offer our praises to God for what He had done. As the fire slowly burned out the rain began to fall upon the campfire area once more. God had fulfilled His purpose for holding back the rains and now He had decided it was time to water His creation there again. We also needed our rest and had to get to bed. We still had one and a half more days of camp left and after this miracle we knew God had great plans still to come.

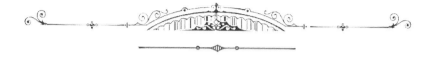

Chapter 15

The last couple days at camp were incredible. Everyone was happy and eager to learn more about Jesus and who God is. It still rained lots, but it didn't affect any of our moods. In fact we all seemed to enjoy it now and created lots of silly rain games and songs. During all the important moments, like our last campfire, the rain stopped just long enough for us to enjoy it and take note that God was watching over us.

God was so alive and real to us all as a result of His miracles. It was a moment I hope none of us would forget. I could also see how everyone else's spirits had come alive and gained a new insight into God and His desire for a closer relationship with each of us.

"Please God, don't let any of us forget you and what you have done for us this week. Please watch over us as we go home and give us boldness to share your miracles with those you need us to." I prayed quietly, as the campers boarded the bus to go home.

The final week of camp for the summer went very quickly and God's Blessings seemed to continue over from the miracles of the previous week. The weather was much better though and everyone was in great spirits, especially the campers. Many lives were changed as a result of how God had renewed our belief in His power and love for all of us, through the trials and miracles of the rainiest week of the summer.

As the final week ended, I was excited to have a few days off once more before preparing for the fall schedule of groups and the cleanup. When I was all packed and ready to leave, Ben asked to speak with me for a moment.

"Malachai, I want to tell you how proud I am of the leader and man of God you have become. I have been watching you closely this summer and how you interact with people. You have a real gift with helping those in need, whatever the need may be. I know how much you have struggled in your own life and I know God has given you an ability to see the world around you in a different way. But, having experiences and knowledge means very little if you don't use them the way they are meant to be. I'm proud of you for how you use everything you are to help others and bring glory to God." Ben shared.

"Wow, thank you Ben. You have been my mentor and friend who I look up to for everything, so this means a lot to me. It isn't always easy either, but something inside me just compels me to do what's right and help others. It's nice to know someone else notices though." I replied.

"You would be surprised how many people notice what you do, but you are not running around looking for credit or a pat on the back, so they quietly thank God for your faithfulness to His purposes. One day you will reap the reward for all you do, but for now just know there are many who appreciate all you do." Ben said.

I took a moment to look around at the beauty of the camp and how the sun was glistening off the lake, before I answered.

"I guess that's why I love this place so much Ben, no matter what force comes against us here, God is allowed to work and we are allowed to be who we are meant to be. I wish I could take this experience everywhere I go, but I know it's just not possible for now." I shared.

"Malachai, I know God has a unique purpose for you and I believe He has already been telling you what it might be. I wouldn't want to lose you from working here at camp, but I also know someone with your abilities and passion for God shouldn't be limited by what this camp has to offer. You have a real gift for working with youth and everything you do and everywhere you go, you seem to bring a joy and hope with you. You also seem to have an ability to make the impossible, possible. God needs people like you to be out there carving the paths and clearing the overgrown trails so that others can find their way to Him once again. It won't be easy, and you'll often stand alone, but it is necessary." Ben stated.

"I understand what you are saying Ben, but it almost feels like you are saying goodbye to me. Has God shared something with you that I should know?" I asked.

"He hasn't shared anything directly, however, I can feel a change in your life coming, a greater purpose. I guess I just want you to know I understand if you can't remain here at camp because God has something more for you. You need to follow His will and purpose, not mine, yours or the camps. If He has been showing you another path for your life, take confidence that He needs you to be there and you need to follow it." Ben answered.

"It's interesting because I've felt the need to move up to the Okanagan but something inside of me is hesitant. I'm actually going up there for the next few days to spend time with my family and see if there is a reason why I should go there. I guess God is getting you to tell me all these things to keep me a little more open to what He has to show me." I said.

"Then you should definitely listen and pay attention. I will be praying for you as well. So I should probably let you go find out what His plans are for you." Ben stated.

"Thanks Ben, for everything." I finished.

I gave Ben a big hug, said goodbye, got into my car and began my trip to see my family and hopefully find out what exactly God had planned as well.

The trip was only a three-hour drive away and from the time I had left the camp until I reached only a third of the way, I felt the presence of something following me. Whatever it was, it kept enough of a distance from me that I could not see or command it. All I knew was that it didn't like me or want me traveling this direction.

As I drove through a portion of the highway where the median in the middle was very deep and wide, and the edge of the road dropped down a very deep valley, I felt the presence grow stronger. I kept trying to focus on the miracles and good times I just had a camp and began thanking God out loud for everything He has done.

However, the more I praised God, the stronger this spirit's anger seemed to become. I knew it had to be close and could sense it was not far above me. I began to wonder if it was the same creature that flew at me while I was at the cabin at the camp. Yet, something seemed different about it still. The only thing I knew for sure was that it didn't like me and that I was driving this direction.

"God please protect me, I want to follow your path for my life and do your will, but I'm scared and need your help. Please, make this spirit leave me alone." I prayed out loud.

Then I spoke a little louder to address whatever this spirit was and said, "I don't know what you want or why you are trying to scare me but I've had enough. I command you through the authority of Jesus the Christ to leave me alone. You cannot stop me from where I need to be." I commanded.

Within seconds, the winds began to pick up heavily around my car and the few trees close to the road began bending sharply as the wind hit them. I felt the anger from the spirit grow incredibly as it came much closer than ever before.

Then I heard another voice speak, "Malachai, put your hands on the steering wheel at the positions of ten and two right now, and hold on tightly."

Suddenly, I felt my entire car get hit by a strong blast of wind, as I heard a loud bang come from my front tire. I began losing control of my steering as pieces from my tire shredded apart and flew off behind me. My car began to swerve sharply to the left where the deep median was, so I held tight to my steering wheel and tried to straighten my car out to avoid going over that edge, but knew there was a long drop over the edge on my right.

It all happened so quickly that I felt I was going to die. I knew whichever edge I went over, there wasn't much of a chance for me to survive. But, I held my hands firmly on the steering wheel at ten and two, praying.

However, just when my car seemed totally out of control and heading for the cliff on my right, I felt something grab my steering wheel with me. Then my car suddenly slowed down very quickly and I was steered safely onto the edge of the road with the cliff just a short distance on the other side of the passenger door.

My tire had completely blown apart, I had no spare, and I was a fair distance from any phone, but I was alive and safe. The anger from the spirit seemed far away now and a presence of peace and calmness now surrounded me.

I just sat there for a moment thanking God for saving me and thanked the angel for steering me to safety.

There weren't any houses along this part of the highway and very few cars seemed to be traveling as well. So I walked to the nearest rest stop where I found a phone to call my mom and brother to help me out. It would take them awhile to get to me and of course now they would also have to stop and pick up a new tire too.

I was still pretty shaken up from the whole ordeal and now I would have to wait for a couple hours before help could arrive. However, there was a small creek beside the rest area, so I found a nice quiet place to relax and think.

I knew this was all an attack against me, but I wasn't sure why. Was it because something didn't want me moving up to the Okanagan? But why? I wasn't sure I was even meant to go yet; however after this, I was even less sure about going. My biggest reason for not moving was still Lucy. I knew we were meant to be together, but I also knew she didn't want to move that far away from her family. If I moved too far away, would she still want to be with me or ever marry me?

I knew I had to do what God wanted for my life, but what if I lost Lucy in the meantime. I also questioned if my life was always going to be in the middle of some spiritual war, should I bring Lucy into it where I would risk her being hurt as well. If this is the kind of attack I get for simply going to visit, what might happen if I lived there?

My mom and brother arrived and drove me to my car, where my brother helped put the new tire on and made sure everything else was safe. We all left at the same time, but I decided to drive a little slower the rest of the way. I was still nervous but just kept thanking God for keeping me alive.

As I drove down the hill just before the bridge that formed the entrance way to my possible new home town, the traffic was very heavy. I noticed a car patiently waiting to get into my lane from a side road just before the bridge. After all I had been through I was feeling very thankful and decided to slow down and let the car pull in front of me.

However, a more impatient person beside me decided to take advantage of the open space and quickly pulled in front of me barely allowing space for the other car to make it in; almost causing an accident. I slowed down even more to allow enough distance for this impatient truck to brake suddenly and not hit the car. After all I had been through already; I didn't want one more thing.

The traffic had slowed even more as we crossed the bridge and I had left a fair distance between the truck and me. However, about two thirds of the way across the winds began to pick up fiercely and I felt another presence around me. I could faintly hear a voice warning me to stay away and I wasn't welcome here.

Immediately after, I noticed the car I let cut in front slam on their brakes to stop quickly, and then the truck in front of me did the same. We were all driving slowly and I knew I had plenty of time to stop, however, when I hit my brakes they didn't work properly. I pressed them as hard as

I could, even pumping them, but they were failing so I skidded my way to almost stopping, and then hit the back of the red truck in front of me.

I was in shock as the driver jumped out to check her truck. Not only had I hit the truck, but also because I had a big heavy car, I pushed the truck into the car that I let cut in front which then touched bumpers with the car in front of her who initiated the panic stop in the first place.

I got out of my car, with a line up of traffic forming behind me and began to apologize to everyone, with tears forming in my eyes. I felt defeated before I even arrived in this city. All the joy I had just experienced at camp was completely gone and I wanted to leave.

The owner of the red truck came over to talk to me, beginning by giving me a big hug.

"Oh honey, it's okay. No one's hurt and it just looks like my bumper and yours are the only things damaged. But everyone's okay." She said.

"I don't know what happened. I had enough room to stop and I tried, but I just couldn't. Plus, just a short while ago my tire blew off on the highway and I almost went over a cliff. I'm really sorry though for wrecking your truck." I shared, with tears streaming down my cheeks.

"Sounds like someone doesn't want you to make it here, I think. But not to worry, everyone's okay and there isn't much damage, so how about we get the cars off the bridge and we can talk about it once we're out of the way of this traffic. You can just follow me to the other side." She said.

Then she talked with the other car owners who decided their cars were just fine and I followed the red truck into a gas station on the other side.

"My name's Elaine." She began saying.

"Hi Elaine, I'm Malachai. Again I'm really sorry about your truck." I said.

"If you're willing to help pay for the damage, then I don't think it will take much to fix. But how are you doing now? It sounds like you've had a rough day." Elaine asked.

"It has been a really rough day. It started good when I left the camp where I work, but since then it has been one problem after another. My mom and brother have already spent half their day helping me once, I certainly didn't need anything else to happen. I'm just really tired and frustrated now." I answered.

"So you do have a place to stay and calm down then, maybe get a drink or something. You seem pretty shaken up still. If you would like, I could follow you to their house to make sure you get there safely?" Elaine questioned.

"I really appreciate it, but I think I should be alright. Their house isn't far from here." I said.

"If you're sure, because I really don't mind. I'll give you my phone number and if you have a place I can reach you at then I can let you know what the cost will be to fix the bumper. But otherwise I recommend you going straight to their house, have a strong drink and relax the rest of the night." Elaine stated.

"Thanks so much for being so kind and I think I might just take your advice, especially after this day." I replied.

When I drove up to my brother's house, my mom quickly came to find out what took me so long to get there. I told her everything else that happened and all she could say was, "I think we should all go inside, have a strong drink and just go to bed before anything else can happen."

As I went to bed, my head was filled with the events that happened during the day. Something didn't want me being in this town and I definitely didn't want to be here anymore either. It was a beautiful place on the surface, but the spiritual strongholds were something much stronger than I was ready to fight. I had been physically and emotionally beaten within one day, to the point of just wanting another drink to forget the events, rather than turning to God for guidance.

This morning I felt on top of the world. Ben was giving me praise for a job well done and my faith in God, now I was exhausted and defeated. If God wanted me to live in this place, He certainly wasn't doing a very good job to convince me it was right. The demons on the other hand were doing a great job convincing me not to stay. I would be much happier being close to the camp and of course Lucy.

I stayed a few more days visiting before leaving back to the camp and work. When I arrived back to the safety of camp I took some time to talk with God.

"I will do what you want me to do God, but I don't think I'm strong enough to fight whatever attacked me. Please, if at all possible, let me stay here where I can still be useful and close to Lucy. I don't want to move up there and have something attack and hurt her too. Besides, how can I be of any use to you if I'm just exhausted and defeated by the attacks all the time? I know you have a purpose for me, but why can't I do it here instead?" I prayed out loud, while sitting on the dock on the lake.

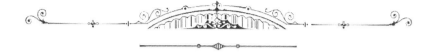

Chapter 16

I had spent the next month working at the camp until my twenty-first birthday, when Ben decided to give me a week off so I could celebrate it with my friends and family. Lucy's parents were letting me stay in their basement so I didn't have to drive back to the camp every night.

I spent my birthday with Lucy and my friends who all made it very special. Darren brought over several different types of alcohol so we could create some fancy drinks to help celebrate and afterwards my other brother took me out to buy me a few birthday drinks at a couple of bars.

I wasn't the type of person to ever get drunk, but I certainly did enjoy trying new kinds of drinks, especially if other people were buying them. The problem I found even though I didn't get drunk, my willingness to drink encouraged others to and they were the ones who often became drunk. My birthday was no different.

The next day however, something had changed. I got up so Lucy and I could head off to church together, but I felt empty and hollow inside. Even as we arrived at church the feeling remained and my anxiousness grew. Something was missing within me; the spirit of God, Himself.

I left the sanctuary of the church and hid in an empty room to pray.

"Where are you? Why won't you answer me? I'm sorry for whatever I did wrong, just please, please God don't leave me alone like this." I desperately prayed.

I felt nothing within me, just emptiness. The presence, spirit of God that I had become so used to was gone. All I could see was darkness within me; the light was gone. When I prayed the words seemed to hit a wall and just echoed back at me. The quiet reassuring voice I had become so reliant on was no longer there and I was left alone with my own thoughts and judgments. Even my ability to see the spiritual had changed; darkness was all I could see. The demons were everywhere I went and no longer cared that I was there. Their looks and sneers made me afraid from the very depths of my soul. For the first time since I had chosen to serve God, I was alone. He didn't have my back. But why, what had I done to deserve this.

For seven days I was cut off from God's presence and left in darkness. Every day I tried to hide from others because I couldn't handle the intense loneliness, fear and darkness that seemed to surround me. I felt hollow and empty, like I was lost in a deep cavern with no light or way out. I prayed constantly, crying and seeking God's forgiveness for whatever I had done or perhaps should be doing to have Him come back to me.

"He's abandoned you Malachai. One simple mistake and your God gave up on you. Now you're left all alone and the others will come to hunt you soon. But, I'm still here for you, willing to help, if you'll trust me." Midnight spoke.

I was in the old wooden saloon once more, sitting in my chair at the table on the balcony. The room was dark and quiet, with the only light coming from the flickering of the candles on a few of the tables. All the people that I was so used to seeing, even the demons that were disguised as servers, were nowhere to be seen. I would have almost believed I was completely alone, if it wasn't for the feeling of fear that ran through my body from hearing Midnight's voice.

"What have you done to me? How are you stopping God from hearing me?" I demanded.

Midnight appeared abruptly in front of me as he slammed his hands on the table, causing the candle to almost fall over. Then his voice became angry as he answered.

"I haven't done anything! You are the one who isn't listening to what He wants you to do! You have chosen to follow your own will rather than His! Don't blame me for what you choose! I came to help and protect you. While your God has cut you off because you won't do what He wants. Even though you constantly turn away from me, I am still here for you. Yet once again I am the one you blame for what God does." He stated.

I moved my chair backwards a bit to give a little more distance between us, and then spoke.

"I'm sorry; I just don't understand what's going on and why. Please, if you really want to help me explain why this is happening? Why has God abandoned me?" I asked.

Midnight stood up to regain his composure, then sat down in the chair across from me. I could still sense his anger, but I didn't feel he was going to hurt me anymore.

"You chose to do His will and gave your life completely to His service because you trusted His purpose for your life. But now you have realized what it means and are starting to understand how much it will cost you. All your own plans, dreams, desires will have to be put aside to do what He wants, when He wants it. Like us, you have no free will, just His purpose. As long as you follow what He wants you will have His blessing and anointing with you. But when you follow your own way or choose your own desires, He removes those blessings and leaves you alone and vulnerable." He said.

"All I did was have a few drinks with some friends, what was wrong with that? The bible says drunkenness is a sin, not just having a drink now and then." I replied.

"Do you really think drinking is what it's all about? He's simply testing you to find out how loyal you really are. He's been telling you to do something and you haven't been listening because you don't trust Him enough and you're scared. And if you don't do what He wants He'll cast you away from His presence because you're not worthy to serve Him. Tell me Malachai, do you really want to serve a master like that?" Midnight asked.

"So this is why you are really here, to convince me to follow you once more. I may be scared of doing what God wants, but I do trust Him still. There have been many times I haven't done what God wants me to do and He has never cut me off from His presence until this time. So there must be a reason why He needed to get my attention this way and now you've helped me realize what it is. The only reason God would cut me off was because He has an important purpose for me to fulfill and He needs me to do what He asks, time is running out." I answered.

Midnight stood up and began to walk towards the stairs, then turned once more, looking directly into my soul.

"You stay loyal to Him even when He cuts you off. Oh, how much I wish you would trust me the same, we could do so much together. Beware though; the path you are following carries much weight, pain and suffering along its way. Many have tried to fight the creatures waiting ahead of you. Many more have tried to walk the path you are on. But very few have ever made it past the first few miles of the journey and even less have survived the war you are entering. You can choose to stay here and let me help you or you can follow His way and most likely die. But remember Malachai, I did warn you." Midnight finished. Then he simply vanished as he began walking down the stairs.

I sat there for a moment in almost complete darkness, just taking in everything Midnight said. How bad would this war really get and was I even capable of fighting whatever the creature was that attacked my car on my last trip.

After a few minutes of sitting there I finally closed my eyes and almost immediately reopened them to find myself lying on the couch in the basement of Lucy's house. It was over but I still felt so alone.

Morning had arrived and I went to church with an open heart ready to hear anything that could help remove this darkness I seemed trapped within. I thought I was doing everything right to be the Christian I was supposed to be. I read the bible, prayed, went to church, served God in so many ways, even gave my very will to His purposes, yet now I just seemed to feel more lost than found.

The service ended and nothing, the darkness was still surrounding me and God wasn't answering. So I got on my knees once more by the pew I was sitting in and prayed.

"I've surrendered to you God and said I would do whatever you wanted me to. I love you and need you, why have you forgotten about me though. If there is something I am doing wrong, just ask and I will do anything you want. But please take this darkness and emptiness from me. I just want your presence back; I need your light. I understand now what hell is, the separation from you and your hope. I don't want to be alone like this anymore, help me please." I cried.

But still the darkness remained.

Defeated and exhausted with trying, I got up and began walking down the aisle to leave, when I heard a voice coming from behind me.

"Malachai, I want you to quit drinking." The voice said.

I quickly turned around to see who was speaking but there was no one around me. The church had mostly emptied out. Just a few people remained and one of the pastors, who is a good friend of mine, was still up at the front, but no one was close enough to speak what I had heard.

"God is that you? What do you want me to do?" I anxiously answered.

Again the voice spoke, this time it seemed to surround me completely. "I want you to quit drinking any alcohol so you can fulfill the purpose I have for you."

I instantly went to the front of the church, knelt down and began crying while I spoke to God.

The pastor came over, placed his hand on my shoulder and asked, "Malachai, are you okay? Can I do anything to help?"

"Pray with me. God wants me to give up drinking any alcohol. I've been so alone all week without His presence, so if He will come back when I do as He asks, then I will do whatever He wants." I answered.

"It sounds like God wanted your complete attention so you would listen. There must be something very important He has for you to do that He would cause you to become this desperate. You are wise to listen, so let's pray." The pastor spoke.

With tears in my eyes, I began to pray, "God I give up my desire for alcohol and any other desire You want me to give up. Please take any want for alcohol from me. I surrender myself and my will once again to You; use me for whatever You need me to do."

Immediately, my soul was flooded with the presence of God once again. My very spirit was being filled once more with light and hope. The darkness was being chased from me like a sunrise pushes back the night itself. I could feel God's love envelope around me. The loneliness was gone and everything seemed brighter once more.

"Thank you God. I will do what you ask." I spoke.

Then I could feel the warmth of God's spirit within me, giving His approval back.

The pastor looked at me, smiled and asked, "God answered you and came back to you, didn't He? Even I can feel His presence around us and you are glowing with the light of His spirit."

"Yes. I'm not alone anymore. I never want to feel what I have this week ever again." I answered.

"Remember, God did all of this to get your attention because He needs you to do something important for Him. You may not understand why He needs you to quit drinking now, but trust that there is an important reason. God has a path you need to follow Malachai and if you choose to follow it He will make everything clear and you will never need to feel the loneliness again." The pastor said.

My heart knew instantly what the next decision was. I had been resisting following what I knew deep down inside I needed to do because I was scared, but now I was more afraid of being separated from God than anything life or the demons could throw at me.

"I think God wants me to move to Kelowna. I don't know why, but it has been on my heart this past month that I'm supposed to. I do have family there, but I don't know what I would be doing, where I would work or how I would live. So I have been trying to make things work out here because it's safe." I shared.

"Sometimes a leap of faith is scary, and following what God wants certainly is not easy. In fact, it often makes no logical sense to us at the time and most won't understand why you choose what He asks. But, if you will trust Him, you will experience much more incredible things in life and see a world few truly understand. In a sense, taking a leap of faith and trusting God to catch you, is like a ship that trusts the lighthouse to guide it safely through the darkness, knowing that its light will help protect the ship from the dangers it can't see on its own. However, it will require you to take action in order to find and experience what could be there, but doing nothing will keep you alone, knowing what you've always known." The pastor said to me.

Humbly, I answered, "Thank you, I think I'm beginning to see clearly once again. I know what I need to do. I guess I should start packing to move and see what God has for me next."

I left the church feeling overwhelmed with everything that had happened, and couldn't help thinking how hard it will be to tell my friends that I needed to move, especially Lucy. However, I was at peace inside about it all and knew this path was right. God was with me once more, so I knew everything would work out somehow.

Lucy and Matt had been waiting for me just outside the main sanctuary and both had a concerned look on their faces as I approached.

"Is everything okay? I know you've been struggling all week with something big, but you seem much more relaxed now. What happened up there?" Lucy asked.

"God's been trying to get my attention, but I didn't want to listen, so He had to do things the hard way. I'm just not sure you're going to like what I have to say though." I answered.

Lucy looked towards the ground and with a sad tone in her voice she asked, "You're going to move aren't you?"

"Yes, but only because God wants me to. Maybe He'll bring you up there sometime as well. I don't want to leave you, but I have to do what God wants and I know you aren't ready to move quite yet. I hope you can understand Lucy. I love you very much and don't want to lose you." I said.

"Are you sure this is what God really wants you to do though?" Matt asked.

"After the week I've just been through, I'm very sure. Let's go out for lunch and I'll fill you in on what's been happening, then I know you'll understand why I have to go." I replied.

We spent the rest of the afternoon together, talking and even praying. In the end they both understood why I had to go and that it was right. I just hoped everyone else would feel the same.

Chapter 17

I was amazed with how God made everything fall into place once I had accepted His will and direction for my life. My friends were all sad I was moving, but they understood why I needed to listen and go. Lucy was taking it the hardest but still found the strength to trust God's plans and purpose for me, so she was my biggest supporter as well.

Ben seemed to already know I was going to be leaving the camp. So when I told him the news and what had happened, he wasn't surprised. He wished I didn't have to leave, but certainly encouraged me to follow God's plans and do what I felt was right.

My oldest brother, his wife and kids were going to let me stay with them until I found my own place. My brother also had some job prospects for me as well. Several other friends were also using their contacts to try to find a job for me as well.

Everything was coming together and in less than two weeks. The greatest part was how much I felt at peace inside. I was definitely nervous and doubts kept trying to creep in, but deep within I had a strong sense of peace that let me know everything would be all right.

Two days before I would be moving, I sat down on the dock for some alone time to pray and just listen to God. The winds began to change direction and blow strongly across the lake. Then large dark clouds started forming in front of me. I could feel the darkness descending, almost circling around me and recognized the strong sense of anger coming from the black cloud directly facing me. It was the creature that came at me when I was on the balcony of the cabin, the one that wanted me to leave the camp.

The cloud began to take the shape of a large dragon-like face, with anger and hatred within its glowing yellow eyes.

"You were better off contending with me compared to what you will face next. I look forward to watching you get all you deserve Malachai. Once you start on this path, you can never turn back. You will either fall or die fighting. Either way I can't wait to see you suffer for all you've done to my kind." The creature spoke.

"I could stay here then and keep contending with you if that would make you happier." I said sarcastically.

"You don't need to do me any favors. I'm more than happy to see you leave. When you're gone I will regain my control here once again. Did God even tell you why He wants you to go and what will be waiting for you?" It asked.

"No, He hasn't. But He doesn't have to either because I know He will be with me and take care of me. Besides I get the impression I will be facing more of your kind there and so far you seem rather easy to control." I answered.

The creature filled with anger and opened its mouth slightly to show its jagged, sharp teeth, and then spoke.

"Don't insult me or my kind any further or we will destroy you and everyone you love. I have been patient with you so far because I knew you would be leaving. But there are far worse spirits waiting for you that will not care who you are and who protects you. You are a vile and arrogant human who deserves no mercy or compassion from our God. Your whole race should die and be forgotten as a mistake, you especially. You think you are more powerful because of your Christ, but without Him you are nothing. You want to be like Him, then maybe it's time to show you how much we made him suffer and hurt too." The creature angrily sneered.

Suddenly, another wind began to flow briskly from behind me. It was strong and powerful but had a sense of calmness and peace within it. It was obvious the creature felt it too as it was becoming very nervous.

I heard another voice speak from within the calming wind as a shape of a man began to form beside me.

"Enough! I listen to no more of your insults and threats. Malachai is with me and you have challenged him long enough. Leave and let your kind know I am with him." The figure spoke, directly to the creature.

"Very well. But this isn't over. Why don't you tell him what's waiting for him and why you want him to go? Then we'll see if he still wants to serve you." The creature stated.

Then, the creature disappeared within the dark clouds once again and the strong wind carried the clouds quickly away towards the mountains. The calming winds began to envelope around me; and the image of a brilliantly glowing man now stood in front of me.

"Malachai, don't be afraid of them or allow them to speak to you in such ways. You are called by the Father to serve His purposes. All who know this and oppose His ways will try to discourage and scare you into giving up. But take courage knowing you are never alone, that is His promise to you." He said.

"I just wish I could see you more though. I can feel you with me, but to see you standing here before me gives me so much more strength to follow what you ask." I shared.

"I know. But it's not enough for you to simply trust in what I can do for you, you need to also believe in what the Father has created you to be so you can fulfill His greater purposes through you." He stated.

"But the only purpose I seem to have is one to pick fights with the demons and be their target to shoot arrows at. I know that's why I was sent here and why I'm being moved again, but each time it gets much harder and I'm getting exhausted. Why can't I have a better purpose like other people do, one that makes people respect me and treat me like someone who's important?" I asked.

He gently put his hand on my shoulder, and then responded.

"Malachai, you still don't realize just how important you really are to His purposes. Of all the people you know who believe and are faithful followers, how many can see and stand up to these demons like you do?" He asked.

"Well, I guess I can only think of a couple who have experienced similar things." I answered.

"Would they stand before the creature like you did today and speak boldly like you have?" He questioned.

"Perhaps not quite as strongly." I said.

"Would they approach demons who are influencing others and command the demon to leave, knowing the people around will question what's wrong with them and judge?" He inquired.

"Well, they might. But I just haven't seen them do it." I responded.

"What about the fact that the demons, including powerful ones like Midnight, know your name personally. Is that something others can boast about?" He asked.

"I'm not sure that is such a good thing though, sometimes I wish they didn't know me." I replied.

"But regardless, they do know you. They may know and be nervous of you at first because they can sense my presence with you and the anointing of the Father upon you, but it is your gifts and boldness that makes them pay attention." He stated.

Then, while turning towards the lake and motioning with His hand for me to look across the water, mountains and sky He continued.

"Look at how perfectly everything works together, the water with all its life; the mountains and all their strength; the sky and all its blessings. Each looks so vast at first glance, but when you look closer you can see how many parts there are working together to make them great and powerful. All the Father has made works the same way. However, when something within these tries to corrupt and destroy, the rest must work together to end the corruption and bring healing and life once more." He shared.

He turned to face me again and while looking directly at me, staring as if to speak into my very soul, He said.

"These demons brought much corruption, pain and destruction into everything the Father created. So He needs those like you who can see the truth, believe and fight alongside the rest of His creation in order to bring the healing back again. The waters are filled with an abundance of life, which He created. Those within the waters live and carry on with their lives barely realizing the greater world that surrounds them at all times. The mountains are where few of your kind choose to climb, but when you do you can see the greater world and some choose to help watch over and protect those in the water. The sky is where the Father and those who dwell with Him watch, protect and provide for all below. We see the greater world from a much different perspective, but know only the Father sees the whole of everything." He said.

"So if I'm on the mountain and I choose to watch over and protect those below, then my purpose is to work with you and the angels to fight the corruption caused by the demons. But in order for me to fight properly I have to climb the mountain higher, gaining a better view and more insight to what's really going on. And the further I climb the closer I reach to the sky and the better I can see you and what your purpose is as well. Is this right?" I asked.

"Yes Malachai, you have much wisdom already, but there is still so much for you to learn. Each person who chooses to follow after the Fathers ways and decides to climb the mountain has a different reason why they start. However, as the journey continues and they endure what they must without giving up, they begin to finally understand what the Fathers true purpose really is. Do you understand what I'm trying to teach you?" He questioned.

"I think so. We can choose to fulfill our own purposes by simply existing within the water and fulfilling our own desires. Or, we can climb the mountain to see a greater purpose beyond ourselves, which will allow us to help others, protect others and change things for the better. Or, we can look towards the sky and work with all of the Father's creation to fulfill His greater purpose itself. It comes down to a choice of serving myself, others or God, right?" I responded.

"Because of your choice, your gift has been opened up and your part in the Father's plan revealed, even to the angels and demons. You have always seen the world differently, but you chose not to deny what you see and allowed the Father to use and guide you. The result is now we can work together to help fulfill His greater purpose and you can become the person He created you to be. You are both a watchman and a warrior, which is why those demons who desire to cause corruption and destruction know and fear you. They will always fight against you and will do their best to make you afraid and give up. But if you stand boldly on what you know the Father has said is right, they will never win." He said, with a power of strength within His voice.

Then He looked toward the sky and a bright beam of sunlight streamed directly down upon us.

"Remember Malachai, everyone has been created to be part of the Father's greater purpose, but until each one chooses to believe, they are merely just a participant and nothing more. When you choose to believe the mountain exists and begin to climb it you start to realize there is a greater purpose and you are a part of it. But once you choose to give up your own purposes and follow the Father's, you can never go back to simply existing within the water or climbing a mountain.

You now know there is so much more and your spirit will never be content with accepting what is less. No matter what the demons or others say or do, you are driven by His purpose and will be able to do all things He asks of you. Never be afraid to do what He asks and walk boldly in the confidence that you are never alone and will be equipped with everything you will need. There are many terrible forces that will come against you, but as long as you serve the Father's purpose, they cannot stop you.

I too am always with you and will never leave you on your own, so go in boldness, strength and peace to fulfill the Father's purpose with your life. You were created by Him and are important and needed; always believe this and accept nothing less. My love is with you and my blessing is upon you always." He finished.

As He spoke these last words, His image faded away into the beam of sunlight, almost becoming one with the sunlight itself. Everything around me seemed to radiate with warmth from the sunlight and my spirit was content and filled with strength and peace.

I knew what I had to do, simply walk in the path that was opened before me and to trust in what felt right within my soul. My own wishes and desires could be deceiving, but trusting that quiet but strong sense of what is right within me told me that this path I was finally following was the way I needed to go. My purpose was no longer to serve others or myself but to fulfill whatever God needed me to do wherever that might bring me.

I know the path ahead of me will not be easy and the demons waiting to attack will unleash their full fury. But I didn't start this war, they did. So as long as I serve God's purpose I know I'm not alone and can do anything He needs me to do.

Made in the USA
Charleston, SC
12 November 2013